CW00506550

Joseph W. Howe

# Winter Homes for Invalids

Anatiposi

Joseph W. Howe

# Winter Homes for Invalids

Reprint of the original, first published in 1875.

1st Edition 2024 | ISBN: 978-3-38282-945-2

Anatiposi Verlag is an imprint of Outlook Verlagsgesellschaft mbH.

Verlag (Publisher): Outlook Verlag GmbH, Zeilweg 44, 60439 Frankfurt, Deutschland
Vertretungsberechtigt (Authorized to represent): E. Roepke, Zeilweg 44, 60439 Frankfurt, Deutschland
Druck (Print): Books on Demand GmbH, In de Tarpen 42, 22848 Norderstedt, Deutschland

# WINTER HOMES

FOR

## INVALIDS

AN ACCOUNT OF THE VARIOUS LOCALITIES IN EUROPE
AND AMERICA, SUITABLE FOR CONSUMPTIVES
AND OTHER INVALIDS DURING THE WINTER
MONTHS, WITH SPECIAL REFERENCE TO
THE CLIMATIC VARIATIONS AT EACH
PLACE, AND THEIR INFLUENCE
ON DISEASE.

BY

## JOSEPH W. HOWE, M.D.,

AUTHOR OF "EMERGENCIES," "THE BREATH," CLINICAL PROFESSOR OF SURGERY
IN THE MEDICAL DEPARTMENT OF THE UNIVERSITY OF NEW YORK, VISITING
SURGEON TO CHARITY HOSPITAL, FELLOW OF THE NEW YORK ACADEMY
OF MEDICINE, ETC.

NEW YORK:

G. P. PUTNAM'S SONS,

4TH AVE. AND 23D ST.

1875.

# PREFACE.

In the preparation of this volume I have endeavored to give a succinct account of the distinctive climatic features of the various winter resorts for invalids, and their influence on disease. The subject embraces such an extensive field that much statistical and other information has been necessarily curtailed, but the principal facts have been enumerated. In addition to the results of my own personal observation in Europe and America, I have investigated the meteorological records, reports of health commissions, and the recorded observations of other physicians with reference to each place under consideration. By this means I have been enabled to arrive at a proper estimate of the value of the different climates in the treatment of disease. The advantages and disadvantages are clearly set forth, so that there can be no difficulty in making a proper selection for each invalid.

J. W. H.

36 West Twenty-fourth St.,
*December*, 1874.

# TABLE OF CONTENTS.

## CHAPTER I.

"Universal Laws" which are not universal—Fallacies of a universal system of treatment—Advantages of a change of climate and the diseases which are cured by it—Selection of location determined by peculiarities of the disease and temperament—Who should go and who should stay at home—Consumption, Asthma, Bronchitis, Rheumatism, Nervous prostration, climate in which they flourish and in which they are cured........................ 1

## CHAPTER II.

### CALIFORNIA.

Peculiarities of soil and climate—Wet and dry seasons—Direction of mountain ranges—Changes in the climate, referable to elevation and exposure to different winds—Months of greatest mortality—Malarial diseases—Rainfall—Range of temperature in winter and summer—Selection of a suitable residence for consumptives—Where to go, how to go, and what to do when you get there—Santa Barbara—Freedom from malarial and contagious diseases—Effects of odor of petroleum—San Diego, San Bernardino, San José, Calistoga, Monterey, San Rafael, and their mineral springs.............. 18

# CHAPTER III.

## FACTS ABOUT FLORIDA.

Diseases peculiar to the climate—Prevalence of malaria in marshy districts—Comparative frequency of malarial diseases in other parts of the Union—Erroneous statements —Climate of Eastern and Western coasts—Wet and dry seasons—Thermal variations—Hygrometric records—The best locations for patients with consumption and Bright's disease of the kidneys—Perils of badly ventilated hotels —Effects of bad food and over-exertion—Selection of a suitable residence — Mineral Springs—Magnolia — Green Cove—St. Augustine—Jacksonville—Enterprise—Pilatka —Tampa.............................................. 38

# CHAPTER IV.

## HEALTH RESORTS IN COLORADO.

Mountain ranges and natural parks—Atmospheric characteristics of various parks depending upon elevation and surroundings—Average range of temperature—Rain-fall —Differences between day and night temperature—Diseases which are relieved by residence in Colorado—How consumptives are affected by the thin air—Danger from hemorrhage—Class of cases to be sent there—Mineral springs of Middle Park—Idaho—Manitou—Environs of Denver, Georgetown, Boulder, Greeley, etc............ 56

# CHAPTER V.

## PINE FORESTS OF GEORGIA.

Thermal characteristics of upland districts—Forests of long-leaved pine—Changes in atmosphere excited by terebinthine odors—Effects on lower orders of animal life and on consumptives—Rain-fall—Average range of temperature—Prevalent diseases—Resorts for consumptives or rheumatic patients—Mineral springs of Sumter county —Catoosa, Madison, etc.—Savannah and its suburbs— Malaria. .......................................... 69

## CHAPTER VI.

### HEALTH RESORTS IN THE CAROLINAS.

Geological formation of South Carolina—Eastern, Middle, and Western regions—Healthy portions of the State —Malarial regions—How the poison may be avoided— Thermal variations — Rain-fall — Pitch-pine forests— Where consumptives should reside—Mineral springs for scrofulous and rheumatic patients—Consumptive patients in Aiken—Environs of Charleston—District of Spartanburg—Slopes of the Blue Ridge—Glen and Limestone Springs—North Carolina—Mineral Springs—Morganstown—Asheville. ............................ 80

## CHAPTER VII.

### HEALTH RESORTS IN KENTUCKY.

Climate of Kentucky—Peculiarities of country—Limestone regions—Agricultural products—Thermal variations— Rain-fall—The value of mineral spring waters in the treatment of diseases—Faith—Diseases which are benefited by bathing in and drinking mineral waters—Mineral springs—Upper and Lower Blue Lick, Big Bone, Mastodon, Paroquet, Olympian, Estele, Crab Orchard, Harrodsburg—Louisville artesian well—Virginia mineral springs. 93

# CHAPTER VIII.

## VARIETIES OF CLIMATE IN THE WEST INDIA ISLANDS.

Northern group—The Bahamas—Peculiarities of location
—Effects of Gulf Stream on the climate—Moisture in
the atmosphere — Variations of temperature — Rainy
seasons—Productions of the soil—Diseases which are
benefited by a residence in the Bahamas—New Providence—Nassau—Harbor and Turk islands—Middle group
—Cuba — San Domingo — St. Vincent — Trinidad — St.
Croix — St. Thomas — Martinique — Southern group—
Curaçoa................................................ 111

# CHAPTER IX.

## BERMUDA ISLANDS.

Coraline formations—Where the zoophytes work—Composition of coral—Soil produced by coral sand and decaying
vegetation—Location of islands—Trade winds—Prevailing winds—Thermal characteristics in winter and summer
—Rain·fall—Prevalent diseases—Annual mortality—Best
months for consumptives and other invalids—What to
eat, drink, and wear—When to exercise—Bermuda, St.
George, Somerset, Ireland—Towns of Hamilton and St.
George ................................................. 128

# CHAPTER X.

## SANDWICH ISLANDS.

Location—Structure of the islands—Thermal variations
at different altitudes—Climate of northern and southern
shores—Effects of trade-winds on climate—Rain-fall in
Hilo and Honolulu—Absorption of moisture by the soil
—Products of civilization—Prevalent diseases—Resorts

for consumptives—Peculiarities of climate in Oahu, Hawaii, Maui—Three principal towns, Honolulu, Lahaina and Hilo.......................................... 140

## CHAPTER XI.

### COLD CLIMATES FOR CONSUMPTIVES.

What class of consumptives require a cold climate—Comparative effects of a warm and cold atmosphere—Care to be observed in the selection of suitable cases for treatment in cold climate—Danger of living in-doors—Minnesota as a sanatarium — Exaggerated accounts of its healthfulness—Topography of the State—Variations of temperature at different seasons—Rain-fall—Mortality among consumptives—Ratio of recoveries—St. Paul—St. Anthony — Minneapolis — Winona — Wabasha—Red Wing—Hutchinson—Ramapo Valley.................... 151

## CHAPTER XII.

### HEALTH RESORTS ON THE MEDITERRANEAN.

The great inland sea—Peculiarities of temperature—Composition, tides, etc.—Northern and southern shores—Prevalent winds in winter and summer—Eastern and western Riviera—Difference in climate between the two portions—Protection afforded by the mountains—The mistral and its effects on invalids—The sirocco, and its disease-laden breath—Prevalent diseases north and south—Dryness of the atmosphere—The Italian sun—Climate of Nice—Sudden thermal variations—Unhealthy conditions of old parts of the city—The time to visit Nice—Woollen clothing—Food and exercise—Monaco—Mentone—San Remo—Corsica, etc.......................... 164

# CHAPTER XIII.

### THE MEDITERRANEAN—(CONTINUED.)

Southern shores—Varieties of climate—Moisture in the atmosphere—Misnamed health resorts—Malarial disorderes —Thermal variations—Sudden changes in temperature— The sirocco—Rain-fall—Location of Pisa—Not the place for invalids at any season of the year—Naples—Difference in climate of east and west side—Sicily—Its physical geography and climate—Principal towns—Products of the soil—Malaga—Algiers—Alicante................ 180

# CHAPTER XIV.

### CLIMATES OF FLORENCE AND ROME.

Florence in a hail-storm—Peculiarities of the prevalent winds—Sunshine—Sudden changes — Location of the city--Malarial fevers—Enteritis—Mean temperature of winter and summer months—Climate not suited for consumptive invalids — Rome — Roman fever — Effects of sight-seeing—Mortality among Americans—Safest time of the year to reside in Rome...................... 191

# CHAPTER XV.

### THE ITALIAN LAKES.

Lake scenery—Peculiarities of lakes on Italian side of the mountains—Variations of climate on opposite sides of lakes—Protection from storms by the mountains—Lake Como—Scenery—Health resorts — Bellagio and Lakes Maggiore, Lugano, Iseo, and Garda................... 201

# WINTER HOMES

FOR

## INVALIDS.

---

### CHAPTER I.

"Universal Laws" which are not universal—Fallacies of a universal system of treatment—Advantages of a change of climate and the diseases which are cured by it—Selection of location determined by peculiarities of the disease and temperament—Who should go and who should stay at home—Consumption, Asthma, Bronchitis, Rheumatism, Nervous Prostration, climate in which they flourish and in which they are cured.

THERE is a growing tendency in the modern mind to make laws as well as to break them. We like to manufacture rules for the mental, moral and physical government of our neighbors. To be allowed to teach them how to eat, drink, sleep, and even how to die, is an admission of our individual superiority. And if our ingenuity is not equal to the task of developing new laws, we quietly resurrect laws from some mummified theories, change their appear-

1

ance by a process of mental patchwork, and present them to those who need to be governed. Few of these so-called laws would bear the light of intelligent analysis, yet the masses accept them without inquiry.

Every profession suffers from one-sided, crude deductions. In the medical world each year witnesses its prolific crop. New "*cures*" are advertised daily. The vegetable-cure, the flesh-cure, milk-cure, water-cure, an army of cures come in from every quarter. Each one has its earnest adherents, with doubtless some foundation for their faith. But they go too far in offering to cure every other sick person on the globe with their special remedies. We know that a diet-vegetarian assists physical growth—that a certain amount of vegetable food is necessary to ward off disease; but to breakfast, dine, and sup on vegetables is not conducive to health or manly vigor. This method of preserving the health would indeed be a wearisome malady. The " milk-cure " has succeeded in many instances. Milk is excellent, nutritious and palatable ; but it does not follow that we are to convert our patients into miniature walking dairies whenever their internal economy is out of order. There is solace to be had from the "grape cure," but grapes do not answer for the treatment of every disease. Because water is known to be beneficial in health and in disease, it is regarded as a panacea for all the ills of flesh. Every patient is "packed," and soaked, and showered. Whether they burn with fever or shake with malarial chills, the drenching process is continued. Young and old, sleepless and drowsy, endure the same treatment, no matter what their special wants or idiosyncrasies may be.

And, again, in the climatic treatment of disease we encounter more "universal rules." Because some consumptives improve in a warm climate, the great majority of sufferers from that disease are allured from comfortable homes to swelter in the tropics, and to endure the cold hospitality of strangers in a strange land. Rheumatic patients are sent to mineral springs, even if the diurnal variations of the temperature of the locality equal thirty or forty degrees. The climatic peculiarities are seldom considered. The composition of the springs alone receives proper attention. And so the same mistaken rules surround and seek to govern every special disease. Men and women are dosed and sent hither and thither, regardless of the distinctive features of each case.

Now we must not be understood as casting a slur on the therapeutical use of any of the substances mentioned among the various "cures," or of abjuring the influence of a warm climate in the treatment of consumption, but we simply deprecate the tendency to make rules of treatment applicable to all diseases.

It is a great mistake to draw the line for all mankind to stand up to. The distinctive individuality of men will not allow such fixed, arbitrary procedures. Men differ as much from each other in their constitutions, temperaments and surroundings— in their likes, dislikes and necessities—as they do in their forms or faces. No one can be a law unto his neighbor. Each man or woman must have the individual separate attention which the special case demands, before either a change of diet or of climate or a drug is recommended.

In the treatment of diseases the value of a change of climate is well understood. Educated physicians of all classes agree that the majority of chronic debilitating disorders may be either relieved or cured by removal to a suitable climate. Drugs, however valuable they may be, are absolutely of less importance in the treatment of certain chronic diseases than the right climatic influences. Among the diseases which are particularly susceptible to a change of climate may be enumerated — consumption, chronic bronchitis, rheumatism, Bright's disease of the kidneys and nervous exhaustion. Many of these diseases which have resisted the most sensible medication succumb to it in more genial climes.

In order to understand the kind of climate best suited to a consumptive, it will be necessary to become acquainted with the history of the disease, the circumstances under which it flourishes, and those under which it is cured. The term consumption is remarkably appropriate. It is derived from a Greek word, φδία, signifying to waste or consume. As a scourge of the human race, it is second only to war and alcohol. Among civilized people in temperate regions it is said to carry off one-tenth of the population. No country is entirely exempt from its ravages. In Iceland the disease is extremely rare, while in the West Indies it is of common occurrence, and is attended by great mortality. These facts show that heat is not a preventive of the disease, and that cold does not necessarily produce it. A damp atmosphere, where the temperature is variable, or a climate so excessively warm as to preclude open-air exercise, poorly ventilated, crowded tenements shut out from the bright sunshine, are all prolific causes of consumption. The disease constantly develops where these conditions exist. Certain occupations also are characterized by a great mortality from consumption. Machine-shops, and manufactories where cutlery is made, increase the length of the death-roll. The minute particles of steel filling the air are constantly inhaled. When they reach the air-cells they produce irritation which eventually terminates in some form of bronchial or pneumonic inflammation. The occupation of mining has a detrimental effect on the health. The darkness, the foul air, and the inhalation of particles of coal combine in developing tubercular disease. One half of the persons engaged in the mines of Cornwall die from consumption. Magendie proved conclusively that the absence of sunlight was a strong predisposing cause of the disease. Extensive tubercular deposits were distinguishable in the lungs of some rabbits which he had confined for several months in a dark cellar.

The people who suffer most from the ravages of consumption are those living in the temperate zone, viz., in England, Holland, parts of Germany, France and America. It deserts the life-giving forests and green fields for the crowded dwelling-places of man. Twenty-five per cent. more die from the disease in town than in the country.

Medicines are of little use in curing consumption. Tonics and cod-liver oil occasionally assist the natural stamina of a patient to overcome the disease ; but they seldom accomplish more than to diminish the rapidity of its progress. The best preventive of consumption, and the most conducive to its cure, are change of habit and of residence, where the principal part of the day can be spent in the open air, under a bright, sunlit sky.

Though a dry, warm atmosphere is suitable for many consumptives, there are some who thrive in a moist climate, or in a steadily cold one—those who like the cold temperature usually suffer much from shortness of breath. They are oppressed and smothered by the hot air of tropical regions. Knowing these diverse natural demands of consumptives, we can appreciate the necessity of a rigid examination of each patient. His habits, his surroundings, his tastes, and the special peculiarities of his disease should be carefully studied. He should be questioned as to the kind of weather which is most agreeable to him, whether dry or moist, cold or hot, and also whether the air of the mountains or the air of the sea-shore is the most agreeable. Then, if the conclusion from the examination is that a dry and warm climate is best suited for the patient, he may choose between Santa Barbara, San José, San Diego, and other places in California; Aiken, S. C.; Santa Cruz, in the West Indies, and Honolulu; or Mentone, and San Remo in Europe. If a warm climate with more moisture in the air is desired, there is Magnolia and St. Augustine in Florida, Bermuda, and Bahama Islands; St. Thomas, and sea-port towns of Cuba, or Corsica and Palermo in Sicily. A very dry and cool climate can be found in Colorado. Those who prefer a climate which is very cold —but, at the same time, without sudden or dangerous changes—will be suited in some parts of Minnesota, in the Adirondacks, and in the Ramapo Valley, in New York State. These places are the principal winter resorts; but there are some others held in esteem, which are described in subsequent chapters.

The patient should take clothing suitable for all changes of weather. Warm climates are sometimes liable to sudden thermal variations, which are injurious to those who are unprepared for them. Cod-liver oil and tonics must be continued. The patient's diet should be regulated according to the special demands of his appetite. The same diet will not suffice for all. Let the patient have vegetables, rare meat, or meat well done, milk or grapes, or in fact any nutritious article of diet which he wishes.

Exercise in the open air is essential. Walking and riding in moderation, at regular periods, stimulates the circulation, and gives renewed vitality. To bathe

1*

every morning with cold water is excellent.  Chilly sensations after the bath may be prevented by rubbing the skin briskly with coarse towels.  This stimulates the circulation of blood in the skin and prevents the chest from taking cold.  If the patient is far advanced in the disease, and more than ordinarily sensitive to changes of temperature, portions of the body may be successively washed and dried— first, the face and neck, then each arm, then the chest and lower extremities.  Bathing should never be omitted, even if it has to be done with a moist sponge under the bed-clothes.  The skin is one of the eliminating organs of the body, and its share of the decaying detritus must be thrown off—otherwise, it will add to the morbific elements, the result of the lung disease circulating in the body.  In addition to the bathing, friction of the surface with the hand, or "kneading" the muscles, is a remedial agent of no little value, in consumption, and in fact in all cases where the circulation is deficient.  In the selection of rooms those which have a southern exposure should be given the preference.  Plenty of sunlight in a room is almost as necessary as pure air.

The sunny side of the house is generally five or six degrees warmer than the north side, and hence is the best for invalids in the winter season.

Asthma arises from a spasmodic contraction of the muscular fibres of the small bronchial tubes. It occurs regularly at certain seasons of the year. A disordered stomach, heart disease, or bronchial inflammation, often excite an attack. Its principal cause, however, is the inhalation of various substances floating in the air. Many are affected during the haying season—hence, that form is known as "Hay Asthma." The odor of flowers, of goats, pigs, cats, of brimstone, smoke and hartshorn have been known to excite it. The attack is usually severe when easterly winds prevail.

There is no one climate that can be recommended for the cure of all cases of asthma. Hot and cold, wet and dry, clear and cloudy atmospheres have each and all proved serviceable. Each asthmatic must select his or her particular spot. This can be accomplished only by experiment. Professor Henry B. Sands, of this city, finds a haven in Halifax, N. S. Henry Ward Beecher seeks his cure in the air of the

White Mountains. Others find out the most crowded, dingy and smoky part of the city, and there succeed in warding off the attack.

Chronic bronchitis is an inflammation of the mucous membrane lining the bronchial tubes. It is characterized by coughing, and a muco-purulent expectoration. It is often associated with consumption and asthma. To perfect a cure it is necessary in nearly all cases to remove the patient to a suitable climate. Climates which suit consumptives are also the best for persons suffering from bronchitis. The same care is likewise necessary in selecting a residence favorable to the idiosyncrasies of the patient. The family physician should decide in all cases as to the fitness of the selection. In conjunction with a suitable climate, the use of mineral water, containing salts of potassium and sodium, will materially assist the cure.

Chronic rheumatism is one of the most intractable diseases with which physicians have to deal. Rheumatism flourishes in damp, cold regions, and where there are sudden and extreme variations of temperature. Every change in the atmosphere, from dry to wet, from heat to cold, produces a fresh attack. Indeed, many rheumatic patients are able to foretell a storm or other unfavorable change in the weather by the unpleasant sensations in their limbs. The expression, " I feel it in my bones," is familiar to every physician.

A change of residence to a warm, dry climate, where the diurnal variations are not very great, will assist in curing the disease. And in making a change it is advantageous to choose a residence near mineral springs containing salts of sodium, potassium, and sulphur. Certain parts of California have a good reputation for the relief their climate gives to rheumatic patients. In Florida, South Carolina, Georgia, Santa Cruz, and in Colorado there are also excellent resorts.

A few years ago the disease of the kidneys, to which John Bright gave his name, was scarcely known. Now it is one of the most frequent ailments on the long list of disorders to which mankind is subject. It is well understood that the disease is on the increase. Where one case occurred ten years ago, there are now twenty cases. Our more accurate classification, arising from greater facilities in the investigation of morbid changes, will account for some of the increase ; but nevertheless there is a real positive accession to the list of sufferers from kidney affections.

Bright's disease is not peculiar to any station of life. Rich or poor, old or young, are alike the subjects of its ravages. Anything which affects the secretory function of the skin—which checks the perspiration—will throw a greater amount of work on the kidneys, congesting them, and in time, if the exciting cause continue, will give rise to a degeneration of the substance of the organ. Exposure to sudden and marked changes of temperature is liable to check the secretion of the skin. Sometimes the breathing apparatus is affected by the internal congestion : then catarrhal disorders occur ; at other times, when the intestines are the seat of the congestion, diarrhœa results, but in many cases the kidneys take the largest share in the morbid changes.

The use, as well as the abuse of alcoholic liquors produces " Bright's disease." The alcohol, in whatever form it is imbibed, is carried off principally by the kidneys, and, in its passage through them, stimulates them to increased action. They become congested, and remain so as long as the use of the poison is continued. In the course of time these repeated congestions produce the disease as in the previous instance. In young children, chronic Bright's disease is engrafted on an acute inflammation of the kidneys, but this class of cases is fewer than any other.

Medicinal agents have very little effect in curing the affection when the exposure to cold and other exciting causes is continued. Patients with this disease specially need a warm climate where the thermal variations are not great. If the patient is so situated that he can use mineral-spring waters, they will be found of benefit. We may mention as suitable sanatoriums, Santa Barbara and San Diego, in California; St. Thomas, Curaçoa, in the West India Islands; and Magnolia, St. Augustine, on Tampa Bay, in Florida. The West India Islands, for Bright's disease, have a more favorable reputation than other health resorts.

Nervous exhaustion, another name for over-work,

is generally the result of close abnormal mental application either in literary or business pursuits. It is characterized by great depression, inability to perform the ordinary duties of life without misapprehension, and tremulousness of the voluntary muscular system. With these, of course, there are various functional disorders — such as dyspepsia, weak sight, neuralgic pains, etc., and it is these which generally bring the patient first under the notice of the physician. It is safe to say that one-half of the business and literary men of New York suffer some time during the year from nervous exhaustion. Many fill premature graves or add to the inmates of lunatic asylums, by their intense eagerness to work and get a step ahead of their neighbors. In this affection medicines alone are of little use. Tonics are sometimes of temporary benefit. The only true course to pursue is to stop work immediately, on the occurrence of the first symptom, and reside in a bracing atmosphere, away from all temptation to continue the labor. The mind as well as the body must have rest. He must be removed from all worry and business entanglements. The only way to get out of the rut of care and anxiety is to run away from it and stay away until there is a complete revolution in thoughts and feelings, and a normal performance of all the functions of animal life. To this class of patients a cool, bracing atmosphere is better than a warm one, although some thrive in parts of Florida and California. Colorado possesses all the attributes of air and scenery necessary to revivify and set rushing anew the sluggish and dammed-up streams of vitality. Minnesota is also a good place to reside in, winter or summer. The mountains of North Carolina or Western Virginia may also be found suitable to the wants of the patient. Whichever place is selected, the patient should exercise daily in the open air, bathe in cold water, if he can do so without being chilled, and if necessary continue the use of tonic medicine until a cure is completed.

# CHAPTER II.

## CALIFORNIA.

Peculiarities of soil and climate—Wet and dry seasons—Direction of mountain ranges—Changes in the climate, referable to elevation and exposure to different winds—Months of greatest mortality—Malarial diseases—Rain-fall—Range of temperature in winter and summer—Selection of a suitable residence for consumptives—Where to go, how to go, and what to do when you get there—Santa Barbara—Freedom from malarial and contagious diseases—Effects of odor of petroleum—San Diego, San Bernardino, San José, Calistoga, Monterey, San Rafael, and their mineral springs.

CALIFORNIA has been an object of interest to the civilized world since the time when it was designated by English geographers as "Drake's land back of Canada." Its luxuriant groves of tropical fruit-trees and spices first interested its discoverers. Later, its glittering treasures of precious metals, hidden in the rock, attracted a tide of enterprising and greedy adventurers. Now it is looming up into prominence as a harbor of refuge for broken-down men and women; for those who have had a surfeit of medicine, and who seek in its pure atmosphere the restoration of their shattered powers.

In California, Nature, " the living, visible garment of God," is seen in " ever-varying brilliancy and grandeur." Its towering mountains, capped with a glittering mantle of snow—its fertile valleys, winding silvery streams—its majestic groves of oak and pine, afford many a picture of unsurpassed loveliness, which the eye feasts on with delight. In no other part of the globe is there such a variety of soil and climate. It is this variety which has attracted so many heterogeneous human elements to its hospitable shores. Within a day's ride, the traveller may experience the rigors of the Arctic regions, the warmth of the tropics, or the moisture and variableness of New York. He can travel over deserts glistening with alkali, destitute of a single leaf, or through a luxuriant Eden of fruits and flowers. In many places, the orange and almond grow up with the cherry, plum, and other northern fruit; and flowers bloom every month in the year.

The upper extremity of California is situated at forty-two degrees; its southern extremity lies about

twenty-two degrees North latitude.   Oregon bounds
it on the north; Nevada and the Gulf of California
on the east; and the Pacific Ocean on the west.
Two extensive mountain ranges, the Coast Mountains and the Sierra Nevada, run in a south-easterly
direction through nearly its whole length.   Between
the two are situated the Sacramento and San
Joaquin valleys.   The principal resorts of health-
seekers are located in Southern California.   They
extend from point Concepcion (where the Pacific
coast makes a sudden turn in an easterly direction)
down as far as San Francisco.

It is not easy to determine the causes which develop the peculiarities of the climate of California.
The differences are so great within the distance of a
few miles that neither elevation, latitude, nor anything else will explain them.

For instance, on the eastern side of the upper
portion of the Coast Mountains, extreme cold and
rain alternate, almost daily, with warm dry weather,
while below Point Concepcion, on the ocean shore,
the diurnal changes are unimportant and the season
is constantly summer-like and equal.   It has been

suggested that the coldness of the upper part is occasioned by a deep-sea current coming down from the north which diminishes the temperature of the atmosphere as it nears the coast, producing cold winds which lower the temperature in the otherwise warm villages beyond the mountains. The eastward curve of the coast at the point previously mentioned prevents the effects of this Polar current from being felt below. At San Francisco the sudden changes produced by this current are very noticeable. During the midsummer months in that city the mornings are often chilly enough to make heavy coats and underclothing desirable, while at noon the thermometer may stand at eighty. These marked changes occur oftener in the summer. In winter the weather along the coast is made milder by the warm current which flows across from the China Sea. Another instance of the remarkable variability of climate is found by comparing Monterey and San Francisco. They are located within seventy-eight miles of each other. During a period of six years the mean temperature of the hottest day at Monterey was fifty-nine degrees F., the coldest mean day fifty deg. making a range of nine degrees only. The average fall of rain and snow amounted to a fraction over twelve inches. In San Francisco during the same period the hottest mean day was seventy-eight degrees ; the coldest mean day, thirty-nine, and the rain and snow-fall about twenty-four inches.

The seasons of California are two, viz., the wet and dry season. The former commences in November and ends in March or April. It is not, as its name would imply, a season of continual rain, but the rain seldom falls except in the winter months ; and even the wet season is full of summer sunshine.

The remarkable equability of temperature, and the bracing atmosphere of many portions of California, make it the centre of attraction for consumptives and those suffering from other debilitating diseases. Medical scientists who have become acquainted with its sanitary value through personal experience, agree in ranking it with, if not above, most health resorts in Europe or America. For consumption especially, the climate of Southern California is admirably adapted. Remarkable cures, even in the last stages

of the disease, are frequently recorded. There can
be found the necessary warmth, combined with a
purity of atmosphere which makes an out-of-door
life perfectly easy and comfortable, with no changes
to affect or frighten the sensitive.

_ Patients, however, must not be sent there indis-
criminately. Only those able to stand the fatiguing
journey should attempt it. To send invalids to die
in a strange land is cruel, and, as we cannot too often
reiterate, it is a most important point to ascertain
which place is best suited to the necessities of the
patient. The climate differs so much that the greatest care should be exercised in the selection of a residence for the patient—his life may depend on this.
Among the places which have an excellent reputation for the cure of consumptives, Santa Barbara
stands at the head.

The county of Santa Barbara occupies a narrow
strip of land on the Pacific coast, extending from
Point Concepcion to San Buenaventura. It runs from
east to west and has a southern exposure. On the
north it is protected from the cold, rain, and winds
of the Pacific by the Coast Mountains. On the

south it is protected from the sea-fogs by the lovely islands lying in front of it. The town of Santa Barbara is situated in a picturesque valley midway between the two points previously mentioned. It is a town of three or four thousand inhabitants, about a fourth of which are invalids. A long, hard, sandy beach, two or three miles in length, affords excellent facilities for sea-bathing or horseback exercise.

Four miles from the town are the hot sulphur springs. Some of these contain sulphur and sulphuretted hydrogen ; others contain alumina, potash, and iron. They are used internally and externally. A large number of persons suffering from rheumatism and various cutaneous diseases visit these springs. Their efficacy is attested by Dr. Riggs of Santa Barbara, and other prominent physicians of the State. Sulphur-spring water should not be used without the advice of a competent physician.

Santa Barbara is a desirable location for invalids. Its climate is unequalled, dry and mild the year round, and free from sudden changes of temperature. In summer the average temperature is below seventy degrees, rarely rising above eighty, while in winter the average is fifty-three degrees. The coldest day during a period of nine years was forty-two degrees. The rain-fall in a year varies from twelve to fifteen inches.

Contagious diseases, such as small-pox, scarlet fever and diphtheria, are never found in Santa Barbara unless brought from a neighboring town. Even then they do not spread. Epidemics which have decimated villages thirty or forty miles distant have left this town untouched. Malarial fevers are also unknown. Many cases of chronic intermittent sent here are cured without the aid of quinine or its kindred antiperiodics. This exceptional immunity from miasmatic and contagious diseases is supposed by Dr. Brinckerhoff to arise from the admixture of petroleum with the naturally pure air of the coast. A short distance from the coast there is an immense petroleum sea-well constantly casting up the crude oil to the surface of the water and covering it for miles. The air necessarily becomes impregnated with it. This theory is plausible, but should not be accepted without further investigation.

2

Consumptives have found in Santa Barbara the health and strength which other resorts failed to give them. In determining on a residence, preference should be given to private houses in the surrounding country rather than to the hotels of the town. The latter are apt to be crowded with invalids, and the associations to a home-sick stranger are not pleasant. Walking and riding in the open air and bathing, are excellent as restoratives, but the patient is apt to overdo them from the renewed vitality and vigor which he feels on his first arrival. Therefore, these good things must be moderately indulged in. The patient should walk every morning after breakfast, and while feasting his eyes on the gladness and beauty surrounding him, he can comfort his lungs with the pure bracing air, unadulterated with smoke, dust, or deleterious gases. After breakfast is the best time for exercise. The weakened frame requires the stimulus of a good meal. In walking, the chest should occasionally be expanded to its fullest extent—slowly, at the same time, the arms should be raised from the sides until they meet above the head, then as slowly lowered until the air is expelled. This practice insures in a short time greater capacity, more breathing power, and consequently less danger from tubercular deposit. Persons, however, who are subject to large hemorrhages should not indulge in this expansive exercise. After a few weeks' residence they may gradually join in the ways of life of those who have made the county their home. If the patient has been taking tonics, cod-liver oil or other medicines suited to the particular complaint, they should not be discontinued. Perhaps in all cases it is well to consult the best resident physician of the town.

Since 1562, when Viciano planted the Spanish flag in the harbor of San Diego, that place has been noted for its mild, salubrious climate. The town of San Diego lies in a capacious bay on the Pacific coast, five hundred miles south of San Francisco. Being one hundred and fifty miles further south than Santa Barbara, it is somewhat warmer. It is not sheltered like the latter, and is consequently liable to sudden changes. The annual rain-fall in San Diego is ten inches. The hottest mean day in a period of six years was found to be seventy-five, and the coldest mean day forty-two degrees F. The days are warmer and the nights colder than in some towns further north. These peculiarities, however, are not incompatible with a healthful climate. The annual mortality is 12.20 to the thousand inhabitants, an extremely small death rate.

Consumptives and asthmatics are the persons most benefited by a residence in San Diego. There is considerable malaria in different parts of the county. Rheumatism is a prevalent disease during the winter months. Persons suffering from rheumatic affections or malaria should avoid it. Invalids should select a residence to the west of the town as near the mountain-slopes as is compatible with their comfort. They must avoid the night air as much as possible, on account of the marked difference in temperature between the day and evening. Flannel underclothing is indispensable, and extra coverings are needed at sundown. Those suffering with chronic inflammations of the throat should not reside permanently in San Diego. They may, however, give it a trial in December and January, and if but little improvement is found, Santa

Barbara may be visited. Fifty miles from San Diego there are hot sulphur springs of considerable value.

There is a lovely town fourteen miles from San Francisco, called San Rafael, which is a fashionable resort in winter and summer. It is about two miles from the western shore of San Pablo bay. The mountains protect it on the west and north, and keep it from the sudden thermal changes which characterize the climate of San Francisco. The air of San Rafael is dry, pure and bracing. It is rarely cold enough in winter to prevent invalids from enjoying the open air every day. The town is reached by steamer from San Francisco.

San Bernardino is not so frequently resorted to as San Diego or Santa Barbara. Its reputation, however, as a health resort is not inferior to the others. The town is situated in a fertile plain, with mountains to the north, west, and east. It is much farther inland than the town previously mentioned, being seventy-five miles from the sea. The air is exceedingly dry and bracing, and very little rain falls during the year. Malaria is almost unknown except in the mining districts. A short distance from the village, situated on higher ground near the mountains, is the site of the old mission of San Bernardino, where invalids are beginning to resort in considerable numbers. Many who have visited Santa Barbara, San Diego, and other places along the route, without relief, have been completely restored to health by the climate of San Bernardino. The same general care and restriction in diet are to be observed here as in other places. There is, however, not so much necessity for avoiding the night air as in San Diego. The hot springs are located four miles from the town, near Mount San Bernardino. Some of them consist of pure water; others contain lime, soda, alumina, and a trace of iron. The principal constituent, however, is lime. The therapeutical virtues of these springs have not been sufficiently tested to enable us to give them a special recommendation. Numbers visit them daily and seem to derive benefit from their use.

Santa Clara valley is another of the attractions of Southern California. Scattered up and down its fertile plains are quiet, lovely nooks, where the sick and weary traveller can find rest and comfort—where he can breathe an atmosphere as pure and bracing and health-giving as any in the State.

The principal resort of invalids in this valley is San José, a small town fifty miles from San Francisco. Although not so warm as Santa Barbara or San Diego, it is well situated for consumptives, many of whom recuperate in a short time. As in other places, preference should be given to quiet farm-houses, where plenty of fresh milk, cream, and butter can be had. But if the milk causes a headache, or other uncomfortable symptoms, it is not well to ascribe it to the climate.

The Congress Mineral Springs are located about thirteen miles from San José. They contain carbonates of soda, iron, lime, chloride of sodium, sulphate of soda, silicate of alumina, and magnesia. The waters are good for rheumatic affections.

*Calistoga*, in Napa county, has been celebrated for some years for the number and variety of its mineral springs. It is a common resort for sufferers from rheumatism, gout, and cutaneous diseases. The springs are scattered over a large extent of country, and are nearly all hot. Their most important constituent is sulphur, free and in various combinations. A considerable number contain iron and magnesia. At the springs large baths are constructed for the convenience of invalids who may choose the special water ordered by their physician.

*Sonoma County.*—The Geyser springs in this county are more valuable than the others in a therapeutical and scientific point of view. To the curious and learned, they afford an exceedingly interesting study. They bubble up through a volcanic paste or force themselves through lava fissures in the rocks through the whole length of the Geyser cañon. Mineral springs of almost inconceivable variety in their composition lie side by side. Among the principal are the Boiling Alum and Sulphur Springs, Black Sulphur, White Sulphur, Steamboat Geyser, and Epsom Salt Spring, Sulphur and Iron, and "Eye-Water" Spring, Iron and Soda Spring, and an acid spring. Many persons frequent the baths, especially in the summer months. The diseases which are benefited by a regular course of the waters are rheumatism, gout, and cutaneous affections. Persons suffering from pulmonary complaints should not reside in the neighborhood.

*Visalia* is situated in the San Joaquin Valley. It is highly spoken of as a resort for invalids, especially for those who prefer dry inland air. It has an excellent hotel, and private boarding-houses in which the sick traveller can find all that he needs in the way of food and attention.

Monterey is about seventy-eight miles from San Francisco in a southerly direction. The climate is comparatively dry and equable. Consumptives who feel invigorated by the sea air may reside here for a few months with benefit. A stage runs regularly from San José to this place.

The Paso-Robles mineral springs are located in San Luis Obispo county, two hundred miles south of San Francisco. The waters are said to be the most valuable in the State for rheumatic and gouty affections, and also for diseases of the skin. The analysis shows that they contain carbonic acid and sulphuretted hydrogen, soda, magnesia, potassa,

2*

iron, bromine, iodine, alumina, silica, and sulphuric acid. Baths are always ready for patients. The springs are reached by steamer from San Francisco to San Luis Obispo. Here a good stage ride of twenty-seven miles from the latter place leaves the traveller at the springs.

We will now take it for granted that the physician has given the patient a thorough examination, and has satisfied himself as to the peculiarities of the disease and the climate best suited to the special wants of the case; that he has also become acquainted with the varied features of the health resorts herein spoken of, and that the patient is ready to start.

California can be reached in two ways, viz.: by the steamers of the Pacific Mail Company, to Aspinwall, thence across the isthmus, by rail, to Panama, at which place, the steamers of the same company take the traveller to San Francisco; or he can across the continent, by the various lines of railroad. The latter is the quickest, but may be tiresome to the invalid who objects to the constant tremor of the cars, or who prefers the sea voyage. The journey to San Francisco by rail may be performed in seven days. Very few invalids, however, can bear such constant travelling by rail—it will therefore be well to divide the journey into four parts, staying over a day at each resting-place. The first part of the journey should terminate at Chicago, a ride of nine hundred and sixty miles, occupying from thirty-four to thirty-six hours. The second stage brings the traveller to Omaha, five hundred and sixty miles from Chicago. A ride of five hundred and seventy-three miles brings the traveller to Sarana, Wyoming territory, a lovely place to rest over twenty-four hours. The next ride extends to San Francisco, where the traveller may spend a day very profitably before proceeding on his journey to the health resort.

There are three principal routes from New York to Chicago, viz.: by the New York Central and Hudson River Railway and Great Western and Michigan Central Railway; or Erie and Lake Shore, and Michigan Southern Railway, or by the Allentown line, which includes the New Jersey

Central, Lebanon Valley and Pennsylvania Central, and Pittsburg, Fort Wayne and Chicago railways. A few hours railroad ride may be saved by taking the Hudson River day or night boat to Albany; thence to Chicago, by the New York Central. A sleeping-car must be had for an invalid on each road travelled. From Chicago to Omaha there is also a choice of three routes, viz.: on the Chicago and North-western, Chicago and Rock Island, Chicago, Burlington and Quincy, and Burlington and Missouri River railways. The time occupied in going from Chicago to Omaha is about twenty-four hours.

From Omaha to San Francisco is a steady ride of four days and nine hours over the Union Pacific, Central Pacific, and Western Pacific railways. At San Francisco the traveller will find conveyances to all parts of the State. San José and other parts of the Santa Clara Valley are reached by the San José Railway from the corner of Market street. Stages from San José run to the New Almaden mines and places of interest in the valley. From San José the cars take the traveller to Gilroy, thence a comfortable stage runs to Santa Barbara, touching on the way the Paso-Robles hot springs, San Luis Obispo, etc.

The Congress Springs are reached by railway from San Francisco to Santa Clara, thence by stage eleven miles to the springs. If the traveller desires to visit Monterey he can go by water from San Francisco, or by stage through a beautiful country from San José.

The trip to San Diego may be made by water from San Francisco, or by rail to San José, and thence by stage via Los Angeles. The stage ride from Los Angeles occupies two days, including an interval of one night's rest at San Juan Capistrano.

The Geyser Springs, one hundred miles from San Francisco, are reached by steamers for the latter place to Donahue, thence by rail to Healdsburg and stage or horseback to Riggs and the Geysers.

San Bernardino is also reached by stage from Los Angeles.

# CHAPTER III.

## FACTS ABOUT FLORIDA.

Diseases peculiar to the climate—Prevalence of malaria in marshy districts—Comparative frequency of malarial diseases in other parts of the Union—Erroneous statements—Climate of Eastern and Western coasts—Wet and dry seasons—Thermal variations—Hygrometric records—The best locations for patients with consumption and Bright's disease of the kidneys—Perils of badly ventilated hotels—Effects of bad food and over-exertion—Selection of a suitable residence—Mineral Springs—Magnolia—Green Cove—St. Augustine—Jacksonville—Enterprise—Pilatka—Tampa.

THE climate of our American Italy has been the subject of considerable misrepresentation. It has been alternately praised and slandered—praised for its mildness and equability, blamed for its swamps and malaria. Only within the past year or two has its paramount claims as a pure, balmy, health-giving climate been fully established. Statistics prepared by careful and disinterested observers have decided the truth of some statements and the exaggerations of others. It is often said, for instance, that malarial fevers prevail to a greater extent in Florida than in other States, and that the mortality from these fevers is excessive, because the air is constantly loaded with mephitic vapors. But the truth is, that intermittent and remittent fevers in Florida are of a milder type, run their course quicker, and are attended by less mortality than in any other State in the Union. These facts were ascertained by Surgeon-Gen. Lawson, who found that in the northern section of this country one in every fifty-four cases of remittent fever proved fatal, in the central sections one in thirty-eight, in Texas one in seventy-five, and in Florida only *one in two hundred and eighty-seven.* It is true there are swamps and "hummocks," where luxuriant vegetation under a hot sun develop miasmatic poisons. These unhealthy spots, however, are only found in great number in the southern portions of the State near the "Everglades." In the north they are few and far between. The greater part of the soil is sandy and covered by immense groves of long and short-leaved pines. These forests constantly exhale a delicious terebinthine vapor which adds to the health-giving properties of the atmosphere. The "hummocks" are patches of land made up of clay and sand and covered by an exceedingly rich and rank vegetation. The laurel, oak and magnolia flourish in these spots, which are always fertile and productive. The clayey nature of the hummock land prevents the water from passing off, and the drainage consequently is imperfect. Hence the prevalence of malaria in their neighborhood.

In this connection it may be remarked that some European authorities give miasm a sort of antidotal power over consumption, and they go so far as to say that no cases are recorded of deaths from consumption among persons who have malarial diseases. Further investigations, however, are needed to give this hypothesis a substantial foundation.

The deaths from consumption in Florida average one in fourteen hundred and fifty-seven, while in Massachusetts the mortality reaches as high as one in two hundred and fifty-four. This of course only includes the resident population. The mortality among visitors suffering from consumption is not very large, but would be still less if physicians, with little knowledge and less conscience, would abstain from sending their patients there in the last stages

of the disease, when every earthly hope of their recovery had gone.    Many unfortunates are sent every
year to Florida with life ebbing out rapidly, and by
men who cannot possibly have an intelligent hope of
their recovery.    Needing nothing but the soothing at-
tentions of the home circle, of sympathizing friends
to comfort them as they pass down the dark valley,
they are torn away, sent on a wearisome journey
to a strange land, among strangers to die.    This
course is so cruel and absurd, that it would almost
seem needless to reiterate the advice previously
given, that only those in the incipient stages of
consumption should venture from a good home
for the uncertainties of recovery in a distant
country.

Florida, with the exception of a hilly portion of
the State near the Georgian boundary, is generally
flat; its highest elevation is not more than three
hundred feet above the sea-level.    In this respect
it differs from the mountainous States we have
already described.    The State occupies the southern
extremity of the Union, and is three hundred and
eighty miles long, extending from twenty-five to

thirty-five degrees North latitude. Although ten degrees nearer the equator than southern Italy, Florida is no warmer and has a far more equable and dry climate. From the geological structure it is evident that the State is comparatively of a recent formation. Through many ages the minute industrious coral-insect was laying in the sea a foundation for the land of the future State to rest on. The lower part of the State, known as the Everglades, is still unfinished, and is not sufficiently reclaimed from the waters to make it habitable or tillable. In time it will doubtless become a substantial dwelling-place.

According to the official weather reports the hottest day in January is seventy-five degrees F.; the coldest, thirty-one degrees F. In July of the same year the highest point reached by the thermometer was ninety-two degrees, the lowest seventy-two. Contrast this July weather of Florida with that of New York in the same month, and the difference will be found to be immensely in favor of the former State. The daily spasmodic jump of the mercury in New York stands out in strong contrast to the comparatively steady, comfortably warm weather of the Southern States.

The average mean temperature of Florida during the past year was seventy-three degrees, and between winter and summer heat there was but the small variation of twenty-five degrees. The annual rain-fall is forty inches. The rainy season occurs during the summer months. In California the so-called rainy season takes place in winter. The greatest amount of rain-fall is in August and the early part of September. In August of 1873 the rain-fall at Jacksonville amounted to seven inches.

Frosts of sufficient severity to destroy the fruit crop occasionally occur. However, the frost is usually so slight as to be scarcely noticeable. The winters are thirty or forty degrees warmer than in New York, and the summer months of the latter place ten or fifteen degrees hotter than in Florida. From the latter part of October to the middle of April, and even later, the air is comfortably warm and subject to few unpleasant changes. Eastern and Western Florida both possess an agreeable climate; the eastern is, however, the more frequented portion.

This is partly owing to the greater facilities for travelling and the better accommodations on the eastern coast. The tropical atmosphere of the daylight hours is tempered by the Atlantic breezes. The nights are invariably cool. Taking it altogether, it is just such a climate as will suit the over-worked of our city folk who need to give their brains a blissful rest, and also for those in the early stages of consumption who feel better in a warm, moist atmosphere than in a cold one. Sufferers from Bright's disease and rheumatism will also find a residence in the vicinity of some of the mineral springs and a moderate use of the waters of valuable assistance to them in obtaining a fresh supply of health and vitality.

Mrs. Abby H. Patton, the original "Abby Hutchinson" of musical fame, says: "This pure balmy air gives one new life; there is nothing like it for the blues, for aches and pains, and the coughs, resulting from New York's raw, wintry wretchedness." Dr. Rogers, a prominent physician of Connecticut, whose ill-health compelled him to give up active service in his profession, and who has resided

in Magnolia for several winters, says: "The climate
is peculiarly adapted for persons suffering from
bronchitis and consumption." Our own experience
in this matter is corroborative of the doctor's.
Several of our own patients, with incipient consumption, have been benefited by a winter residence
in Florida; two have completely recovered. Yet,
with all its advantages, it does not seem to possess
so favorable a climate for the great majority of
consumptives as certain parts of California. The
objection to the latter place is the length of time it
takes to get there. Only those in the possession of
considerable vitality can risk the fatigue of the
journey, while Florida can be reached by water in
a short time and with little exertion.

Among the many invalid resorts Magnolia offers
somewhat better inducements for a winter residence
than other parts. Magnolia is located in one of the
healthiest districts in the State. It has a sandy soil,
covered with beautiful groves of pine and orange-
trees. There are no dangerous hummock lands near
the hotels and cottages. The village is on the west
bank of the St. John's river, a short distance from

the celebrated Green Cove Springs. Oranges and other tropical fruits are plentiful. Careless strangers are prone to over-indulge in these luscious edibles until brought down with diarrhœa or other affections of the intestinal tract. A moderate indulgence does no harm. The winter months at Magnolia are remarkable for their mildness and freedom from sudden thermal variations. Rainy days are few. The days are always warm and the nights cool. There is a first-class hotel there, with several fine cottages in connection. Cottage-rooms are preferable to hotel-rooms, as the former are usually more comfortable and home-like, and the circulation of air is better.

The invalid, on first arriving in Magnolia, must not indulge in too much active exercise. Getting over-heated in a warm climate before being acclimated is apt to be followed by intestinal inflammations. Rowing, horseback exercise, and walking are all good and conducive to health, when taken in moderation—injurious otherwise. If the patient is equal to it, a walk or horseback ride to the springs of Green Cove daily, and a bath and draught of the waters, will be of great advantage in the cure of Bright's disease or rheumatism. Even for consumptives such a course might be beneficial. In all cases it is well to consult the resident physician before indulging in all the enjoyments of the place. The physician, usually, is acquainted with the good as well as the unfavorable elements of the place, and his advice may be the means of warding off many evils.

The Green Cove Springs are much frequented by persons broken down with rheumatism and gouty affections. A few consumptives also reside there. The village, like Magnolia, is located on the west bank of the St. John river, at a point where the river is four miles wide. It is about four miles and a half from Magnolia. The springs are a short distance from the river, and cover an area of thirty square feet. The water has a temperature of seventy-six degrees Fahr. It is used both for bathing and drinking. It contains sulphates of magnesia and lime, chlorides of sodium and iron, and sulphuretted hydrogen in considerable quantities. Comfortable bathing rooms are attached to the springs. Respecting the number of baths necessary, one each day may be taken with benefit. More than this should only be indulged in by the advice of a competent physician. The quantity of water drunk must depend on the disease, and should be regulated by a medical man. Patients too often do themselves incalculable injury by incessant "tippling" at the springs.

There are several pretty cottages and a commodious hotel, in which visitors for pleasure and health can find comfortable accommodations.

St. Augustine, from its antiquity and historical associations, is one of the most interesting cities on the continent. Its record is full of thrilling events. No town in the United States has experienced so many vicissitudes, has passed through so many ordeals of fire and sword. Its walls are cemented with the blood of its enemies and defenders. Four times within the last three hundred years it has been completely destroyed. It was first destroyed by fire by the Huguenot De Gourges, who slaughtered the whole Spanish garrison in revenge for the slaughter of his Protestant countrymen, in the French settlement, at the mouth of the St. John river, a year or two before. Later, in 1566, the British Admiral

Drake landed, sacked the town, and drove the Spaniards out. Seventy-five years later the city was again destroyed by Davis. It was burned again by Moore in 1702. In 1743, Oglethorpe whipped the Spaniards, and made considerable havoc in the palaces of the Dons. During the rebellion its streets were the scenes of riot and bloodshed. At the commencement of the war it was in the hands of the Confederates, but soon afterwards the Union troops entered and held the town until the proclamation of peace.

St. Augustine is located about fifty miles south of the St. John river, on the Atlantic coast. The island of Anastasia lies in front of it, and separates it from the ocean. The city consists of comparatively small houses and narrow streets. A concrete stone called *coquinia*, a combination of powdered shell and sand, is used in building. The general aspect of the place savors more of the Old World than the New, and shows at once its antiquity.

Since the time when Ponce de Leon, the Spanish visionary, landed at St. Augustine in search of the famous spring of everlasting youth, this region has

3

been noted for its health-giving qualities. It is protected from miasm by the salt marshes around it, while the cool air from the ocean tempers its tropical heat, and renders it a very desirable residence for invalids. The climate during winter and summer is equable, neither too hot nor too cold. The summer's noonday heat is not greater than the heat in some parts of Canada and Northern and Middle States. All winter the days are warm without being uncomfortable. The amount of moisture in the air is not very great. There is more moisture in the air at St. Augustine than at Magnolia. Those who find that element in the air agreeable and beneficial should try a residence in the former place. The average range of temperature in the month of January was seventy-five degrees F., in July it was eighty-one degrees. The yearly mean, by one observer, is given at sixty-nine degrees.

Private lodgings in this, as in other resorts, are preferable to the hotels. The traveller can find in St. Augustine many quiet houses, in which cheerful accommodations may be had at reasonable figures. There can be no objection to the hotel, however, if well-ventilated rooms can be secured. The old hotels in the town generally lack all the requisites of a healthy residence, and, unless they are improved, they should be shunned under all circumstances.

Jacksonville is the largest town in Florida. It lies on the west bank of the St. John, and is the centre of the enterprise and business of the country. It is about thirty-five miles from the mouth of the river, and is in communication, by steam and rail, with all parts of the Union. The town derives its name from General Jackson, whose efforts to subdue the Seminole Indians in Florida are well known.

The thermal variations are much the same as at the towns previously mentioned; the highest temperature in July, 1872, was ninety-three degrees F., the lowest seventy degrees, the highest temperature during the month of January is given at seventy-five degrees, the lowest forty-one deg. F.

In the town and suburbs there are excellent accommodations. A residence on the outskirts at " La Ville," or Riverside, is more desirable than in the town; both places are well situated and contain comfortable places of abode. Some prefer the vicinity of Jacksonville as a winter-home because of the society which it contains. But independent of its life-bustle and constant intercourse with Northern ports, it is not so well suited for invalids as places previously mentioned.

Enterprise is acquiring some reputation as a residence for invalids, especially for those suffering from rheumatism. It is further south than any of the resorts spoken of in previous pages. It is pleasantly situated on the east side of the St. John's river, on the borders of lake Monroe, at the head of navigation. There are two places called Enterprise, viz., the Old and the New. Old Enterprise is about a mile higher up the river than the new village. The latter place is in the vicinity of some magnificent orange-groves. The country surrounding the southerly resort has greater beauty and interest. The day temperature is several degrees higher than at Magnolia, and the nights are nearly as cool. Winter is like our northern May and June. The annual rain-fall amounts to fifty inches. Within a short distance of the village there is a large mineral spring, the principal ingredient of which is sulphur. It is eighty feet in diameter,* one hundred in depth, and as clear as crystal to the bottom. No analyses of its waters have been made, and its medical virtues have not yet been tested. There are great facilities for fishing and hunting within a few miles of Enterprise. Persons addicted to those sports make this town their headquarters.

Pilatka is nearly one hundred miles from the mouth of the St. John. It has an excellent location on high ground, on the west bank of the river. The surface land of the district is for the most part sandy. There is little or no mal aria in the vicinity. Although Pilatka has all the climatic advantages of other health resorts on the river, it has not as yet become much patronized by invalids. The winter months are delightfully warm and the rainy days are few. The nights are generally cool enough to allow of a comfortable night's rest. There are good hotels and private cottages where the traveller may be ac-

---

* Bell's Florida.

commodated with either a temporary or a permanent residence.

Western Florida to the health-seekers of the North is as yet a comparatively unknown region. The means of communication are far behind those of the eastern portion. Accommodations for travellers are also inferior in every respect. It has, however, a fine climate—a climate that is warmer and somewhat drier than the eastern side. The rain-fall is less in amount and the diurnal variations of temperature are not so great or frequent. Frosts are extremely rare. During the winter of 1874, Mr. Samuel H. Clapp of this city spent several months travelling in this part of the State. He speaks in the highest terms of the salubrity and health-giving properties of the climate. He thinks Tampa Bay is destined to be, in the future, one of the principal health resorts in Florida. This bay is situated at about the centre of the State, opening on the Gulf of Mexico. The harbor has a capacity sufficient for vessels of the largest size. The surrounding land is sandy. For miles along the shore a beautiful tropical vegetation exists. Large groves of orange, lemon and pine-trees are everywhere to be seen. The best months to visit this point are January, February, and March.

Notwithstanding the fact that Tampa Bay possesses many of the requirements of a first-class health resort, we would not recommend it as a permanent winter residence, because of the lack of comfortable lodging-places in and near the village. It is difficult to provide food and other necessaries suitable for the fastidious palate of invalids.

Cedar Keys, in twenty-eight degrees north latitude, has a fine climate for rheumatics and consumptives.

# CHAPTER IV.

## HEALTH RESORTS IN COLORADO.

Mountain ranges and natural parks—Atmospheric characteristics of various parks depending upon elevation and surroundings— Average range of temperature—Rain-fall—Differences between day and night temperature—Diseases which are relieved by residence in Colorado—How consumptives are affected by the thin air—Danger from hemorrhage—Class of cases to be sent there—Mineral springs of Middle Park—Idaho —Manitou—Environs of Denver, Georgetown, Boulder, Greeley, etc.

Though Colorado was known to the Spaniards three hundred years ago, its first entrance into civilized history dates from the exploration of Zebulon Pike in the beginning of the present century. Subsequently, Long and Fremont added something to the general knowledge of the territory. It is only, however, within the last fifteen years, that its topography and climate, and its vast mineral and agricultural resources have become fully and widely known.

Colorado has had its successes and reverses like

other new territories. The frenzied rush for the treasures in its rocky bosom, transformed the hard-working emigrants into lawless hordes anxious to achieve a fortune in a single day. But in time the exaggerations vanished, and a stampede of weary, disappointed men, half emptied the State. But in their place came a steady, hard-working people who have made a substantial foundation of prosperity for themselves, by developing the mineral creations of ages and giving them a reliable and permanent value.

The State occupies nearly the centre of the Great West, between latitude thirty-nine degrees and forty-two degrees North. In the same latitude, in the Eastern Hemisphere, the southern portion of Italy is situated. Colorado is bounded on the north by Nebraska, on the east by Kansas, on the west by Utah, and on the south by New Mexico. The widest range of the Rocky Mountains passes through the State from north to south. It measures two hundred and sixty miles from east to west. It occupies a greater elevation above the sea-level, and has a more salubrious climate than any of its

3*

neighboring States or Territories. Its topography is peculiar. Its valleys and table-lands are as far above the sea-level as ordinary mountains are, and its mountains tower far above the altitude of the great mountain ranges of the north; yet in these lands of the air there is a glorious profusion and richness of vegetation seen nowhere else in the world at the same level. In the White Mountains, at the height of seven thousand feet, vegetable life is almost entirely absent, while in the Middle Park of Colorado, at eight thousand feet, cereals and the richest flowers grow, and cattle are pastured in the open air most of the year.

In the Alps, at a similar height above the sea-level, the mountain sides and plateaus are covered with snow; wet and rainy weather prevails, and vegetation is remarkably scanty. In Colorado, the days of winter are like a northern summer without its changefulness, and the summer is but little warmer than the winter. The air is very dry and bracing. The nights are nearly always cold—in fact, so cold that winter clothing is essential for comfort. The peculiar dryness of the atmosphere of Colorado, and its generally equable climate, are due to its location in the centre of the continent—to its elevation and the shelter given it by "Nature's monuments"—the mountains. They temper the icy breezes of the north and steal their moisture.

It must be borne in mind, however, that this healthfulness of climate is not peculiar to the whole State. It belongs to certain elevations, and mountain slopes, and valleys. High up in the mountains, and in unprotected districts, the fiercest storms rage, and variable, rainy and cold weather prevails. The mean daily temperature of the eastern slope of the mountains during one year, as reported by the United States Signal Service, was forty-seven degrees Fahr. The hottest mean day was sixty-nine degrees Fahr. The rain-fall for the same period was about sixteen inches. In New York, one degree further north, the rain-fall in the same period reached forty-five inches.

As the air is exceedingly thin and dry, it is apt to cause considerable discomfort to a stranger, making the head light and exciting slight hemorrhages from the mucous lining of the nasal cavities and bronchial tubes.

Bayard Taylor states that new-comers may be rec-

ognized by the spots of blood upon their **hand-
kerchiefs.**

The whole eastern slope of Colorado and the southern portions of the natural parks are remarkable for
their fruitful soil and invigorating atmosphere.
These parts are suited to consumptives, asthmatics,
and persons suffering from nervous exhaustion.
Only those in the incipient stages of consumption
should reside in this State. When the disease has
progressed to the second stage—softening of the lung-
tissue—there is a great tendency to hemorrhage,
and, as the air excites bleeding even in healthy persons, it would be disastrous to such patients. In
fact, it is no uncommon thing for consumptive
invalids to faint from loss of blood a few days after
their arrival. But there is no danger if the stranger
is in the first stages, or if he is free from hemorrhages.
If, after a couple of weeks' sojourn, he should not experience a marked improvement in every respect, a
change should be made to Santa Barbara, or other
parts of California. Whether it would be safe for
the patient to take the journey must entirely depend
on the condition of his strength. If he should be

very weak, it would be better, perhaps, for him to choose some one of the lower valleys at the foot of the mountain.

Persons afflicted with disease of the heart, or anything else which predisposes to congestion of the lungs, should seek another climate.

Asthmatics can live comfortably in any settled portion of the State. They generally find immediate relief from the disease in any of the habitable places in the parks or on the mountain slopes. If, however, they do not experience immediate relief they must go elsewhere. Those suffering from rheumatic and gouty affections should select homes near the mineral springs of the Middle Park, Idaho or Manitou.

Winter clothing and warm bed clothes are indispensable. The material difference between the temperature of the day and night will injuriously affect the sick and well unless they are prepared for it.

The natural parks of Colorado are at the present time the centres of attraction for tourists of every nation. They consist of the North, Middle, South,

and San Luis parks.    Their evergreen hills and
dales, their exhilarating, bracing breezes, and pure
air, are rapid restoratives of the sluggish mind and
feeble body.   They are not, however, places for persons who are *broken* down, but only for those who
are *breaking.*

The Middle and South parks are more extensively
known than the others, and are best suited for invalids.

Middle Park is located in Summit county.   It is
about seventy miles long and thirty wide.   Its entrance is about one hundred miles from Denver City.
It is encircled by mountains, some of them among the
highest in the world.   Long's Peak, the highest, is
said to be as high as Mont Blanc; and Lincoln's
Mountain is only a few feet lower.   The principal
object of interest for the invalid in this place is the
Hot Spring, near the banks of the Grand River.
This consists principally of sulphur, free and in combination.   Bowles, in his " Switzerland of America,"
thus speaks of them :

" On the hill-side, fifty feet above the Grand
River, and a dozen rods away, these hot, sulphurous

waters bubble up at three or four different places within a few feet, and coming together into one stream,
flow over an abrupt bank, say a dozen feet high, into
a little circular pool or basin below.    Thence the
waters scatter off into the river.    But the pool and
the fall unite to make a charming natural bathing-
house.    You are provided with a hot sitz bath and
douche together.    The stream that pours over the
precipice into the pool is about as large as would
flow out of a full water-pail turned over, making a
stream three to five inches in diameter.    The water
is so hot that you cannot at first bear your hand in
it, being 110° Fahrenheit in temperature, and the
blow of the falling water, and its almost scalding
stream, send the bather shrieking out, on his first
touch of them ; but with light experiments, first an
arm, then a leg, and next a shoulder, he gradually
gets accustomed to both heat and fall, and can stand
directly under without flinching ; and then he has
such a bath as he can find nowhere else in the world.
The invigorating effects are wonderful.    There is
no lassitude or chill from it, as is usually experienced
from an ordinary hot bath elsewhere.    Though the

water be 110° warm, and the air thirty to forty degrees cold, the shock of the fall is such a tonic, and the atmosphere, strictly, so dry and inspiring, that no reaction, no unfavorable effects are felt, even by feeble persons, in coming from one into the other. The first thing in the morning, the last at night, did we renew our trial of this hot bath during our brief stay in the neighborhood, and the old grew young, and the young joyous and rampant from the experience."

These hot springs are admirably adapted to cases of rheumatism, scrofulous skin diseases, and nervous prostration from over-work. It must be remembered that invalids cannot stand as much as well persons; and that in any case the bathing and drinking should be done in moderation.

South and San Luis parks are much warmer than the Middle Park, and better suited for the former class of invalids. But the journey over the mountains to suitable villages in this lonely spot is so hard, that only those who are possessed of considerable strength can undertake it.

Idaho is seven or eight miles from Central City.

It is situated in a lovely valley, in the Rocky Mountain portion of Clear Creek Valley. The village has an elevation of eight thousand feet above the level of the sea. Little rain falls during the year, and the air is remarkably dry, pure, and bracing. The principal attraction of the place is the hot springs. These contain sulphates of soda, magnesia, iron, and lime.* The waters are used principally for bathing. In selecting a residence near the springs, care should be taken to find one in a protected situation, and to get a room with a southern exposure. The nights here, as in other portions of this elevated district, are extremely cold, so that extra clothing is always necessary. When easterly winds are blowing, invalids must remain in-doors.

Manitou is a small village located near the Mountain Cañon, not far from Pike's Peak. It is in a charming situation. The mountains protect it from the cold winds, and shade it from the glare of the noonday sun, which is apt to be disagreeable. It is shady, but has plenty of sunshine.

The town is rapidly increasing in size from the

---

* Mineral Waters of America, by Walton.

influx of wealthy Englishmen and Americans, who find here a sufficiently healthy climate to meet their various needs. It is the summer-home of Mrs. Lippincott, well known to all Americans as " Grace Greenwood." Mrs. L., in her "Western Letters," says : " There is no such air out of heaven for asthmatics as in Colorado, and especially at Manitou." One of the attractions of Manitou is the mineral springs, an analysis of which has not yet been made. They are known, however, to contain a large proportion of sulphur, while one or two contain soda in various quantities.

A steady course of bathing in the water, in connection with their internal use, removes rheumatic and gouty pains, while the stimulating air removes catarrhal affections of the nasal and bronchial mucous membranes, and gives renewed vitality to the whole system. Asthmatics and persons having a consumptive tendency, without hemorrhage, will find a residence at Manitou of great benefit.

The same general measures for protection from cold and attention to ordinary hygienic rules are also necessary here.

Some persons in bad health have found a residence in or near Denver City to be of benefit.

Denver is the principal city of Colorado. It is in Arapahoe county, and about fifteen miles from the foot of the mountains. It has an elevation above the sea-level of four thousand feet. The scenery around Denver is magnificent. Nearly two hundred miles of the mountain range is visible, including the two principal giants of the State, Pike's and Long's Peak.

A residence in the town is not advisable. Suitable accommodations can be had in the suburbs.

Should the traveller wish to test other places he can remain in Boulder, twenty-five miles from Denver, or in Georgetown, forty-five miles distant. Some like the location of Greeley, fifty miles off. This town was started by the agricultural editor of the *New York Tribune.* It has progressed with great rapidity, and now numbers a population of 2,000 souls.

Part of the route to Colorado is the same as that to California. The traveller may take any of the routes mentioned at page 55, to Chicago or Omaha.

From Omaha the Union Pacific Railway runs to Cheyenne, a distance of five hundred and sixteen miles. There the Denver Pacific line carries the traveller to Denver, and from there stages and cars run to all the resorts previously mentioned. Middle Park Springs are reached by railway from Denver to Golden City, thence to Georgetown by stage and over the Berthoud pass into Middle Park by horseback. Idaho is reached by cars to Central City and stage six miles to the springs.

# CHAPTER V.

## PINE FORESTS OF GEORGIA.

Thermal characteristics of upland districts—Forests of long-leaved pine—Changes in atmosphere excited by terebinthine odors—Effects on lower orders of animal life and on consumptives—Rain-fall—Average range of temperature—Prevalent diseases—Resorts for consumptives or rheumatic patients—Mineral springs of Sumter County—Catoosa, Madison, etc.—Savannah and its suburbs—Malaria.

THE pine forests of Georgia are a continuation of the great belt of pine which extends from Virginia to the southern extremity of Florida. In Georgia these magnificent forests cover a larger area than in any other State. The air is loaded with the soothing, balsamic aroma exhaling from their countless pores. Manufacturers of turpentine and resin are looking to these grand groves to supply the ever-increasing demand for these products which the rapidly disappearing northern forests inadequately supply.

The long-leaved pine is the principal species of pine in Georgia. It is sometimes inaccurately desig-

nated as yellow pine or pitch pine, as these names
belong to other species. The long-leaved pine is
technically recognized as the *pinus palustris* and
*pinus australis*. There are other varieties here,
such as the pinus tæda or loblolly, but the principal
growth consists of the pinus palustris. Pine trees
usually grow on sandy soil. They reach a height of
eighty or ninety feet, and have a diameter of from
one to three feet. Crude turpentine is the vegetable
juice of this tree, and also of various species of larch
and fir. It is obtained by making incisions in the
bark, and catching the drainings in vessels prepared
for the purpose. The exudation consists of a resin
in combination with a volatile oil. When separated,
this oil is known as the oil of turpentine, so univer-
sally employed in the arts and sciences. It is used
medicinally both internally and externally. When
taken internally in small doses it increases the secretion of all the mucous membranes. It has a stimulating effect on the kidneys, augmenting the flow of
urine, and in some cases (if given in large doses)
it is likely to cause strangury. The drug has also
some reputation as a remedy for tapeworm. When

applied to the cutaneous surface it produces a reddening and tingling—hence its use as a counter-irritant.

Pine grove localities have the reputation of being very healthy. There is usually complete freedom from malarial and pulmonary diseases. Iron will not rust in these woods as rapidly as in other places. The terebinthine odor exerts also a peculiar effect on the development of the lower orders of animal life. They are rarely found to exist in pine groves, and their number is increased only by migration. The atmosphere, impregnated as it is with the peculiar volatile principle of the trees, has a soothing effect on inflamed throats and irritable lungs. Strangers on their first visit often experience a tendency to strangury, but, as a rule, the air agrees with everybody. Invalids with troublesome coughs and shortness of breath, rapidly improve after a short residence, and some far advanced in tubercular disease recover their health completely. The dryness and mildness of the atmosphere has, of course, something to do with the beneficial effects experienced, but there is no doubt whatever that much of the benefit arises from the air being impregnated with the "piney" odor.

The pine woods of Georgia extend from one end of the State to the other, along the eastern and middle sections. They commence about seventy miles from the eastern coast. That portion of the State bordering the ocean is partially made up of tide and swamp lands suitable for the growth of rice. The cotton islands fringing its borders make an excellent breakwater, which gives a safe, protected channel along its whole extent. In the interior the land consists of a rich sandy loam. The northern part of the State is mountainous, is rich in minerals, and the soil is considered good for the different cereals. The southern parts of Georgia are the healthiest; still, many of the northern towns are much visited and esteemed by invalids. As in California, there is in Georgia every variety of soil and climate. The cool, bracing air of the north may be found in its upland and western districts, and a balmy, dry atmosphere, tempered with cool breezes, in its southern districts. Tropical fruits and flowers grow up together with the fruits and flowers of the Northern States. The winter days are bright, mild and sunny, with little variation in the temperature. The mean temperature in December and January is about fifty degrees Fahr. In midsummer it is eighty degrees Fahr. The average rain-fall is estimated at fifty-five inches. These observations were made at Augusta. Further south the temperature is somewhat higher.

Savannah and its environs are visited during the winter months by those in search of warmth and health. The city is seventeen miles from the mouth of the Savannah River, and occupies an elevated and commanding situation. In point of artistic beauty, it is second to no other city in the Union. Its streets are regular and arranged at right angles to each other. Lofty evergreen trees line the sidewalks, handsome squares and plazas contain lofty pines, evergreen shade trees, and beautiful walks fringed with bright flowers, blooming nearly the whole year. These breathing-spots, and the general healthfulness of the city, make it a desirable residence during the winter season. Pulmonary diseases, such as consumption, bronchitis, etc., are not so common as in our Northern cities. Malarial af-

4

fections are rare. The average mean temperature is sixty-six degrees Fahr. In winter the days are warm and but little rain falls. There are no marked or sudden changes. During the summer Savannah is a much pleasanter residence than New York, the temperature seldom or never reaching the point it does in this city. This equable summer climate results from the cool winds coming in from the sea. Invalids who require the comforts, the society, and recreation which can only be obtained in an important city will be satisfied with Savannah. There are numerous hotels and private boarding-houses, on or near the principal parts, which are fitted with all the modern appliances. Monument square, or Jasper and Forsyth parks are desirable localities for consumptives. In the suburbs there are also attractive and healthy homes, where strangers are accommodated. The invalid should spend the first few days in Savannah quietly. Overmuch sight-seeing is not conducive to health, and many are irretrievably injured by it. The out-door exercise should be taken at separate intervals during the day, and is better after meals than at any other time. Riding

on horseback is better an hour or two after eating.
No violent exertion is good when taken too soon after
meals. Strict attention to diet must also be en-
joined, and especially during the first week or two
of the patient's sojourn. Augusta is, in the winter
months, another favorite resort for invalids. The
city is located on the banks of the Savannah, two
hundred and thirty miles from its mouth. It occupies a high bluff, and, although at the head of navigation, the river is very wide, and both shores are
picturesque and attractive. The sanitary advantages
of Augusta are not superior to those of Savannah,
although a larger number of invalids make it their
home. The streets of Augusta are wide and beautiful. They are lined by rows of commanding trees,
between which in many places are grass plots. The
air is dry and delicious. The thermal variations are
not marked. Consumptives receive benefit in a
short time, if they do not task their strength by im-
moderate exercise or over-eating. Persons suffering
from nervous exhaustion, or who are worn-out generally from excessive work, will find Augusta a desirable winter residence. In the city and suburbs

are good lodging-places, and no comfort that money can procure need be denied the sick. Some persons prefer to divide their time between the two cities, spending the first part of the winter in Savannah, and dwelling in Augusta through the months of February, March and April.

Marietta is a small village near the Kenesaw Mountains. It has a fine healthy location, and beautiful surroundings. In the summer time it is visited by the opulent citizens of Atlanta, who prize its sanitary advantages. The Northern tourists and invalids, who have visited this village and its environs, speak highly of the dry, bracing atmosphere of this locality. In the course of time it will probably be more widely known.

The Warm Springs of Meriwether county are the most valuable mineral waters in the State of Georgia. They are situated in a picturesque section of country near the Pine Mountains, and are surrounded by numerous pleasant walks and drives. The principal spring contains oxides of magnesia and calcium, protoxide of iron, carbonic acid and sulphuretted hydrogen. The properties of the spring are both alterative and tonic. Another valuable spring in the same vicinity has entering into its composition sulphates of soda and magnesia, and a large quantity of sulphuretted hydrogen. There is a cold spring containing iron and a large proportion of free carbonic-acid gas. The waters of the warm springs are used for both drinking and bathing. The diseases cured by their use are chronic rheumatism and gout, syphilis and scrofulous skin diseases. Overdoses of the waters sometimes produce violent headache and purging. At first small quantities should be taken and then gradually increased until the system is perceptibly affected. The atmosphere in the neighborhood is clear and bracing, and doubtless tends as much to bring about a restored condition of the vital functions as the mineral waters.

The springs are reached from Columbus by a stage-ride of thirty-five miles. The latter place is about one hundred and twenty miles by rail from Macon.

The chalybeate springs of Talbot county are located about seven miles south of the Warm Springs. They are much employed for the cure of anæmia and general debility.

The Red Sulphur Springs of Walker county have a reputation for the cure of rheumatic affections and skin diseases. The springs are twenty in number, and occupy an attractive region near Lookout Mountain, at the base of Taylor's ridge. This portion of the State of Georgia contains some of the choicest scenery in the world. The air is cool and bracing in summer time. In winter it is mild the greater part of the season. The springs of course are the principal attraction for invalids. A quantitative analysis of them has not yet been made. They all contain sulphates of magnesia and soda, sulphuretted hydrogen ; one or two contain iron, and hence are employed for their tonic effects.

In Catoosa county there are some valuable mineral springs, about four miles from Ringgold, on the Western and Atlantic Railroad. They are reached from the latter place by stage. Previous to the war these springs were visited by large numbers of invalids annually, but since then the patronage has diminished, and the buildings have been allowed to get out of repair. Still, there are good accommodations for all who choose to visit them.

The major part of the springs contain as a principal ingredient iron in various combinations. A few have a large proportion of sulphur.

The Madison springs of Madison county are situated a few miles from Athens. Neither a quantitative nor a qualitative analysis has yet been made; they are said to contain sulphur and its compounds in large quantities.

The time occupied in the journey from New York to Savannah by rail, is fifty-four hours; by steamer it is sixty hours. There are three lines of steamers, which send boats on Tuesdays, Thursdays, and Saturdays from New York.

# CHAPTER VI.

## HEALTH RESORTS IN THE CAROLINAS.

Geological formation of South Carolina—Eastern, Middle, and Western regions—Healthy portions of the State—Malarial regions—How the poison may be avoided—Thermal variations—Rain-fall—Pitch-pine forests—Where consumptives should reside—Mineral springs for scrofulous and rheumatic patients—Consumptive patients in Aiken—Environs of Charleston—District of Spartanburg—Slopes of the Blue Ridge—Glen and Limestone Springs—North Carolina—Mineral Springs—Morganstown—Asheville.

THE Palmetto State before the war occupied an enviable position. Her marvellous agricultural and mineral resources were being rapidly developed, and her citizens enjoyed the gratification of a constantly increasing prosperity. Unfortunately the war of rebellion, and evil political influences since, have sadly blighted her hopes of prosperity.

There is, however, in many parts of the State, strong, healthy reaction. Business, in some of the seaport towns, is steadily increasing. In some places, where there has been constant and direct communication with the north, and where Northern capital is supplied, there has been complete recovery, a renewed , life, and there can be no doubt that South Carolina, so rich in soil and minerals, will once more recover its old prosperity.

The greater part of the eastern coast of the State is low and swampy, and is used principally for the production of rice. The cotton islands, upon which grow the famous sea-island cotton, front this part of the State. Farther inland the country is still flat and uninteresting. Towards the west and north it gradually rises, until the Blue Ridge Mountains are reached. This portion and the sandy uplands, covered with pine, are the driest and healthiest in the State. In many respects it has a climate resembling Southern Europe, without any more sudden variations in the daily temperature than are noticed there. Both the Carolinas are good winter resorts, but they are objectionable in the summer months. Malarial fevers prevail then along the eastern coast, the margins of streams,—in fact over all the low and damp regions of the country. In some of the principal seaports yellow fever sometimes occurs, either sporadically

4*

or epidemically. There has been no serious epidemic of that disease for some years. The rainy season also occurs in the summer. Heavy and frequent rains are common, and the air is loaded with moisture. From these causes the climate is not suited as a summer residence for Northerners, except in the extreme northern and western portions of the State. During the winter there is very little rain ; the days are usually cloudless and warm. The diurnal thermal variations are greater than in Florida. Between the day and night temperature there is often a difference of twenty degrees. Hence, invalids must pay great attention to their clothing, and provide suitable winter dresses for day and evening wear. Consumptives generally improve faster in the high lands of the western part of the State than in the counties bordering on the Atlantic. However, there are some who prefer the moister and lower lands, and who do well there. Rheumatic and gouty patients may reside anywhere in the neighborhood of the mineral springs. Those afflicted with malaria will do well to seek a residence in some other State, but they may derive benefit from the climate of the northern slope of the Blue Ridge Mountains. The Fall and Spring months are the best seasons to reside in South Carolina. The latter part of December, January and February, consumptives who are beyond the incipient stages will do well to go further south into Georgia or Florida. March and April are exceedingly mild in South Carolina, and very free from disagreeable variations.

Aiken is the principal centre for consumptive invalids in the Southern States. But like many other, places its advantages are often over-estimated. Those who have come away from it benefited, extol the virtue of the climate, while the unfortunates, who have not been relieved, express their thorough dissatisfaction with it. The town, however, both in its location and surroundings, is well suited as a winter home for those in the incipient stages of tubercular disease, and also for rheumatic and gouty patients. It occupies a high sandy ridge near the Edisto and Savannah rivers, and in its vicinity there are beautiful groves of the long-leaved pine. The air is clear and mild. On some it has a stimulat-

over-work, who are nervous and unstrung, will find the climate of this valley particularly beneficial. In the surrounding country, as game is abundant, there is excellent hunting and fishing, and there are quiet little villages where tired folks can rest and obtain comfortable lodging-places among a hospitable people.

Sullivan's Island, near Charleston, is now quite a resort for pleasure-seekers. It is said to be a most desirable place for invalids. In winter many Northerners reside on the island. Some of them, great sufferers from rheumatism, say they find the climate to be agreeable and well suited to their special afflictions.

*North Carolina* furnishes some remarkably salubrious localities for the broken-down and over-worked. Its mineral springs also furnish vital pabulum for rheumatics. North Carolina has its sister State and Georgia on the south—Virginia and Kentucky on the north; its eastern coast is on the Atlantic. Like South Carolina its territory may be divided into three portions, viz., a coast region, low, in many parts covered with pine; a middle district, hilly and dry, and the western region, which is mountainous.

The middle and western portions of the State are the healthiest—up among the mountains and along the slopes of the Blue Ridge. The air is cold and stimulating.

The climate has none of the characteristics of Florida or of the southern parts of its sister State. In winter the atmosphere is cold and contains but little moisture, and is free from sudden variations. The mean temperature of the middle section of the State is sixty-six degrees; the mean summer temperature seventy-five degrees, and the temperature during the winter months is forty-three degrees. The annual rain-fall is forty-five inches. These high regions have been found to suit that class of consumptives who need cold bracing air, without dampness, or excessive diurnal variations. It has not the intense coldness of Minnesota or the Adirondacks, and is therefore better fitted for the class of cases we speak of than either of these regions. Asthmatics also receive benefit here. Some leave completely cured. The north and north-western sections are

good resorts for invalids suffering from nervous prostration. They can exercise in the mountain air daily.
Either walking or riding is good for them and for
other patients able to bear out-door life without too
much fatigue.

Morgantown, in the high western portion of the
State, is one of the oldest towns in the county. It
lies in a commanding situation on the slopes of the
Blue Ridge Mountains, in Caldwell Co. It has an
elevation of eleven hundred feet above the sea-level.
The scenery at various points near the town is said
to be exceedingly beautiful. During the winter the
days are cold and the air contains but little moisture.
The nights are always cold. Fine drives can be
taken all through the surrounding country on good
roads. All who prefer dry mountain air will be
satisfied here.

A few miles from Morgantown there are some
excellent mineral waters. They contain sulphur and
iron in variable quantities, and are said to possess
diuretic, tonic and alterative properties. As yet,
however, they are not much visited—on account of
the limited accommodations for travellers in their

vicinity. In time they will doubtless become familiar resorts for invalids of all classes.

Asheville is another interesting village situated in a lovely valley near the French Broad River. It possesses all the natural advantages of a cold, dry health resort. Comfortable homes can be had, suitable for both invalid and tourist. This is a railroad and stage centre. Travellers come and go to all points. Stages leave Asheville every morning for the warm springs on the banks of the French Broad River. They are justly celebrated all over the State for their curative properties. Many intractable cases of chronic rheumatism have been cured by them. The temperature of the springs varies from ninety to one hundred and three degrees. Their chemical composition has not been accurately ascertained. They are known, however, to contain carbonic acid, carbonate and sulphate of lime and magnesia. There are other springs in this neighborhood also having some therapeutical value.

The Shocco Springs of Warren county enjoy some favor in the treatment of chronic skin diseases and rheumatism. They contain sulphates of soda and magnesia, and sulphuretted hydrogen. They sometimes produce profuse diuresis. To reach these springs the traveller will go by rail from Raleigh to Warrentown, and from the latter place a stage-drive of nine miles will take him to the springs.

# CHAPTER VII.

## HEALTH RESORTS IN KENTUCKY.

Climate of Kentucky—Peculiarities of country—Limestone regions—Agricultural products—Thermal variations—Rain-fall—The value of mineral spring waters in the treatment of diseases—Faith—Diseases which are benefited by bathing in and drinking mineral waters—Mineral springs—Upper and Lower Blue Lick, Big Bone, Mastodon, Paroquet, Olympian, Estele, Crab Orchard, Harrodsburg—Louisville artesian well—Virginia mineral springs.

THE climate of Kentucky is not suitable for consumptives or those who are much debilitated by grave disorders. The changes of temperature are often sudden and extreme, and exert a prejudicial effect on weak and sensitive organizations. The State, however, is considered extremely healthy. The winter, though cold, is short. In the north and north-eastern portions of the State it lasts about three months; in the south it can scarcely be said to exist over two months. The seasons of spring and autumn are very mild and agreeable. The thermal variations, as obtained by the United States Signal Service at

Louisville, show the mean temperature of January to be thirty-one degrees, of July seventy-nine degrees Fahr. The rain-fall is estimated at thirty-eight inches. The atmosphere all over the State is considered very pure and bracing. It is well adapted to those who are overworked and who much need a change of air and scenery. In the south-east portion of the State the country is mountainous and wild, affording excellent opportunities for enjoying the beauties of nature and the sports of the huntsman. The western part of Kentucky is undulating, hilly and fertile. The limestone regions are the most productive in an agricultural point of view.

Kentucky is visited yearly by large numbers of invalids, who seek a restoration of health by the free use of the mineral waters which abound in all parts of the State. The medicines furnished by mother earth are daily growing more and more fashionable. People have greater faith in them than in the products of the laboratory, and faith, though not recognized by authorities as a remedial agent, is nevertheless a valuable adjunct in the treatment of all forms of disease. And when in addition to this faith they reside in a bracing atmosphere, are regular in their habits, and have complete rest from work and worry, there is really very little for the mineral waters to do. Fully appreciating as we do the value of mineral waters in certain diseases, we cannot but feel that too much importance is attached to their daily use as well as to the use of other medicinal agents. A judicious system of advertising and puffing is at the bottom of the reputation of many of the mineral springs in this country and in Europe. Men who know little of disease generally, discover their hidden virtues. They advertise—hire a chemist to make an elaborate analysis, and a physician to make a report of the diseases which it cures, and little time passes before invalids crowd to the place with exaggerated expectations. It would be strange indeed if some of them were not benefited, and many doubtless are. But the promiscuous dosing of old and young with mineral waters, no matter what diseases affect them, is unqualifiedly wrong, and productive of great physical harm. The family physician is the one to decide whether the patient should visit the springs, and not the proprietor, who has everything to make and nothing to lose by the visit. The diseases which are cured by the administration of mineral waters are few. A brief reference to them will be necessary in this connection. In rheumatic affections there is usually an excess of lactic acid in the blood, which manifests itself by exciting inflammation in the fibrous structures of the joints. Alkalies are given to counteract the effects of this acid, and they can be administered in no better way than as they flow from the natural fountains of the earth. Bathing in warm saline waters, also, diminishes the acidity, and when followed by a brisk rubbing, stimulates the circulation so much as to remove the congestions around nerves and joints, and establish an equilibrium in the circulating fluid. Then the fresh pure air which usually exists in the locality of the springs also adds to the patient's stock of vitality, promoting digestion, and preventing the mal-assimilation which produced the acid. Gouty affections also are relieved by the use of saline waters. But before any special benefit can accure to the patient, he must regulate his diet, and refrain from the use of alcoholic stimulus. Waters and medicine fail to effect a cure while Nature's laws are outraged. The mineral spring waters which contain an excess of sulphur with salines, are much used in the treatment of lead and mercury poisoning. In lead-poisoning specially the internal and external use of sulphur water is valuable. The lead in the system combines with the sulphur, and is thrown out through the various emunctories. In the various forms of scrofulous skin diseases, mineral waters are often prescribed without reference to the special wants of the patient, hence the bad results which constantly occur.

Hard drinkers, whose abdominal viscera are congested by the excessive use of alcohol—who are bloated and covered with the papular rash of rum —are more benefited by a systematic course of saline waters than any others. Five or six weeks of hard drinking at the springs, instead of the bar, will re-move the general plethora—relieve the liver and bowels of their congestion, and give tone to the digestive functions. When there is a watery condition of the blood, with general debility, mineral waters containing iron are sometimes beneficial. Iron increases the

5

quantity of red globules in the blood, besides giving tone to the stomach—hence the efficacy of waters or preparations containing the metal. Alkaline waters are of great use in certain affections of the kidneys and bladder. In the incipient stages of Bright's disease, or when the kidneys are not eliminating a sufficient quantity of metamorphosed nitrogeniz- ed material from the blood, these waters are always good. When the solid constituents of the urine are deposited in the form of gravel, a moderate use of salines will be of benefit. The deposit disappears sometimes from the first doses of the waters, but, on discontinuing them, reappears, so that a prolonged course of the waters is necessary for permanent re- lief. The mineral waters containing an excess of soda and potassium are the best for cases of gravel. Small quantities should at first be administered, the doses being very gradually increased until the system is affected.

We have no faith in the treatment of paralysis by mineral waters. There is no harm, however, in trying them, especially in the form of baths, which by stimu- lating the circulation may assist in bringing about a successful termination of the disease. But the bath can generally be had at home ; there is consequently little use in taking a paralyzed patient from the comforts of home to the disquietude of a hotel among strangers.

Kentucky is famous for the abundance of her mineral springs. The encomiums bestowed on their curative properties by physicians have placed them on the list of valued therapeutical remedies. On the margin of the Licking River, in Nicholas county, are several important springs respectively denominated as the. Upper and Lower Blue Lick Springs. The Upper Blue Lick Springs are about twelve miles from Maysville, in a fine healthy country. The waters are employed both for drinking and bathing. They have a slight cathartic and diuretic action. In congestion of the liver, rheumatism and gout, they are employed with considerable benefit. From Judge and Fennel's analyses, as given in Dr. Walton's "Mineral Springs," we learn that their ingredients are carbonates of magnesia and lime, chlorides of potassium, sodium and magnesium, sulphates of potash and lime, iodide and bromide

of magnesium, alumina, peroxide of iron and silicic acid.

These springs are favorite resorts of Western people, but the accommodations for travellers are not
the best in the world. Improvements, however,
are being made.

The Lower Blue Lick Springs have also a good
reputation. The early settlers in the region cured
their venison with the salt which crystallized on the
margin of the springs. The largest spring at this
point is close to the river's edge, and is about five feet
deep. An analysis of those waters by Dr. Peters
shows that they possess a similar chemical composition to the Upper Blue Lick Spring. They are
used for gout, rheumatism, syphilis and scrofulous
skin diseases.

In Boone county there are several valuable
springs. The principal ones are the "Big Bone,"
"Mastodon," and "American Epsom." They are
located about seven miles from Walker, on the Louisville and Cincinnati Railroad. It was in this neighborhood that remains of the extinct mastodon, an
animal of the elephant species, were discovered.

The principal ingredients of those springs is sulphur. They contain in varied quantities sulphuretted hydrogen, chloride of sodium, sulphates of magnesia, soda and alumina, bicarbonates of lime and magnesia, and carbonate of soda. These waters are specially adapted to the treatment of skin diseases both syphilitic and scrofulous. Persons who are troubled with looseness of the bowels must partake of these waters with great caution. The effects of small doses should be noticed before the quantity is increased.

The Paroquet Springs, in Bullitt county, are located a few miles from Shepherdsville. According to the analysis of Prof. I. L. Smith, they contain carbonates of soda, magnesia, iron and lime; chlorides of potassium, sodium, magnesium, and calcium; sulphates of soda, alumina and lime; iodides of sodium and magnesium, silica, carbonic acid and sulphuretted hydrogen. From this analysis it is readily seen that these waters possess valuable therapeutical properties. They are much used in the treatment of kidney affections, rheumatism, gout and cutaneous affections. Some physicians recommend them in chronic inflammations and diseases of the intestines.

The Esculapia Springs of Lewis county are also employed in skin and kidney diseases. They excite all the secretions, but especially increase the action of the skin. In the majority of cases their diuretic and diaphoretic action is well marked. Sulphur is their principal ingredient, although they also contain in small quantities lime, magnesia and sodium in combination with carbonic acid and chlorine. In the same neighborhood there is a good chalybeate spring, the waters of which have been found efficacious in the treatment of general debility accompanied by anæmia.

A few miles from Mount Stirling, in Bath county, are the celebrated Olympian Springs. The neighborhood of these springs is one of the finest in the State. The country around is wild, hilly and picturesque, and, independently of the mineral waters, is a good place to spend a few weeks. The air is cool and delightful, and agrees with most visitors. There are three principal springs, the most inportant of which has been analysed by Dr. Peters. He found carbonates of magnesia and lime, chlorides of potassium, sodium, and magnesium, sulphide of iron, bromine, alumina, silica, carbonic acid and sulphuretted hydrogen. This spring flows at the rate of six gallons per minute. The diuretic action of the water from this spring is equal to the others. Hence it is frequently employed in the treatment of chronic affections of the kidneys and bladder. Of the other two springs in this locality, one is known as the Black Sulphur Spring, and the other contains iron. Neither of these latter are much used by invalids.

The Estill Springs comprise several varieties. They are located in Estill county. The principal purgative spring is the "Irvine." It contains carbonates of lime, iron and magnesia. Its principal ingredient is sulphate of magnesia, ordinarily known as "Epsom Salts." The waters are employed for obstinate constipation, congestion of the liver, and to relieve plethora. The sulphur springs of this region are known as the Red, White and Black sulphur springs. An analysis of the "Red" shows that its constituents are sulphates of potash, soda, and magnesia, sulphuretted hydrogen, carbonates of soda, magnesia, and lime, chloride of sodium, silica and carbonic acid.

The third spring of the Estill group contains more of the salts of lime and magnesia than sulphur, and also more carbonic acid gas. It has a strong diuretic and alterative action.

The Crab Orchard Springs are situated in Lincoln county. The waters of these springs contain large quantities of magnesia and lime. The "Crab Orchard salts," * which are much employed in the West instead of Epsom salts, are manufactured from these springs. An analysis shows that the water contains in one hundred parts *sixty-three* of sulphate of magnesia, four parts of sulphate of soda, and four parts of chloride of sodium or common salt. There are also minute proportions of lime, iron, silica and bromine. As is readily seen by their constituents, these springs have a cathartic action. They are used principally in obstinate constipation and torpidity of the liver.

Harrodsburg Springs is the favorite summer re-

---

* Walton.

sort of the Kentuckians. The country is exceedingly attractive and healthful. The village and springs are about thirty miles from Frankfort. The waters contain carbonates of iron and lime, sulphates of magnesia and lime, and chloride of sodium. They have a laxative effect, and are employed in constipation, dysentery, and congestion of the portal system.

*Climate of Virginia and Mineral Springs.*— The State of Virginia possesses a salubrious climate. Only the south and south-easterly portions, made up of lowlands, suffer from malarial disease. During the summer the mountainous regions of the State, and especially those where mineral springs exist, are thronged with visitors from all parts of the Union. Of course the springs are the principal attraction. They are among the most valuable in the world. The Greenbrier White Sulphur Spring has an excellent reputation for the cure of dyspepsia, constipation, skin diseases, rheumatism, and Bright's disease. The springs are located in a valley surrounded by the Greenbrier Mountains. Although on apparently low ground, the spot is two thousand feet above

5*

the sea-level. The temperature of the mineral waters is about sixty-two degrees Fahr. They contain carbonates of lime and magnesia; chlorides of sodium, magnesium, and calcium; sulphates of soda, magnesia, and alumina; iron, sodium, sulphuretted hydrogen, oxygen, nitrogen and carbonic acid.* Walton says they resemble in composition the sulphur waters of Neuendorf, in Electoral Hesse.

These waters are alterative, diuretic, and cathartic. The family physician or the resident physician at the springs should always be consulted with regard to the quantity to be taken internally, and applied in the form of baths. In some forms of consumption and disease of the heart, they often do positive injury; therefore the advice of competent physicians is always necessary.

In Monroe county, Virginia, there are a large number of valuable springs. The most important are the Red Sulphur Springs, which possess a peculiarity of composition and therapeutical action not found in

---

* Walton.

other waters. With the ordinary ingredients, such as carbonates and sulphates of soda, lime and magnesia, they contain a peculiar compound of sulphur and organic matter. Prof. Hayes, in his report of the analysis of this substance, says: " The peculiar sulphur compound which forms a part of the saline contents of this water has never been described, if it has ever been before met with; while in the natural state and out of contact with atmospheric air it is dissolved in the water and forms a permanent solution. Air, acids, and other agents separate it from the water in the form of jelly and alkaline carbonates; alkalies, water, and other agents redissolve it. It has no acid action on test-fluids, but bears that character with bases, and forms compounds analogous to salt. In its decomposition ammonia is formed, and hydro-sulphuric acid is liberated; or, if heat be employed in the experiment, sulphur is separated. It combines with the oxide of silver, and forms a salt of a reddish-purple color, in the form of a flocculent precipitate which dissolves in pure water, with the oxide of lead, a yellowish-white powder, and with the oxide of copper a pale blue salt in fine powder. Mixed with a small quantity of water and exposed to a temperature of eighty degrees F., it decomposes and emits a most offensive odor of putrefying matter with hydro-sulphuric acid.

These waters have a sedative effect. They reduce the frequency of the heart's action, and are hence useful in all diseases when the action of the heart is abnormally increased, either in force or frequency. They are also said to be beneficial in pulmonary complaints, such as chronic bronchitis and chronic pneumonia. They act by diminishing the congestion of the mucous membrane, and allaying irritation. In large doses the waters have a cathartic and diuretic action.

In the same county there are also the salt sulphur, sweet sulphur, and iodine springs, which are much employed in diseases of the liver, especially those which arise from the excessive use of alcoholic stimulants, skin diseases, and syphilis and scrofula. The waters containing iodine are particularly applicable to syphilitic and scrofulous diseases, and many sufferers are relieved by drinking and bathing in the waters.

The Yellow Sulphur Springs of Montgomery county are also much used. They contain magnesia, iron, lime, soda, potash, and alumina in various combinations. The springs are located on the east side of the Alleghany Mountains, in the midst of wild and beautiful scenery. There are facilities here for bathing as well as for drinking.

The chalybeate sweet springs of Alleghany county are much employed in diseases which impoverish the blood, such as anæmia, chlorosis, and exhausting discharges. Warm baths can be had daily.

The alum springs of Rockbridge county and the alum springs of Pulaski have a beneficial action in chronic diarrhœa, dysentery, night sweats of phthisis, and profuse leucorrhœa. They are remarkably astringent in taste. They consist of chloride of sodium, sulphates of potash, magnesia, and lime, iron, alumina, chromate of ammonia, silicate of soda, sulphuric acid, silicic acid and carbonic acid.

In one half-tumbler dose six times each day these waters have a strong diuretic action.*

---

* Walton.

The regions occupied by these various mineral springs, although mainly resorted to in summer, are good places to spend the winter months. All those who like a cold bracing atmosphere, and a lovely country, will receive benefit anywhere among these mountains.

# CHAPTER VIII.

## VARIETIES OF CLIMATE IN THE WEST INDIA ISLANDS.

Northern group—The Bahamas—Peculiarities of location—Effects of Gulf Stream on the climate—Moisture in the atmosphere—Variations of temperature—Rainy seasons—Productions of the soil—Diseases which are benefited by a residence in the Bahamas—New Providence—Nassau—Harbor and Turk islands—Middle group—Cuba—San Domingo—St. Vincent—Trinidad — St. Croix — St. Thomas—Martinique —Southern group—Curaçoa.

As the West India Islands cover an area of three thousand miles and extend from ten degrees to twenty-four degrees North latitude, and have every conceivable variety of geological conformation, it necessarily follows that the climate must vary. Some are healthy—others are unhealthy. One island possesses an equable, dry and warm atmosphere, another a moist and changeable one, and yet another an equatorial climate, burning and dry, which none but those born and bred there can bear. It will, therefore, be only necessary, to describe the prevailing characteristics of certain islands which are suitable for invalids and the diseases which are favorably influenced by their climate.

First on the list we find the northern group of islands, commonly known as the Bahamas. Like most of the other West India Islands, they have had an eventful history. The irrepressible Spaniards first took possession of them shortly after their discovery by Columbus in 1492. San Salvador or Cat Island was without doubt the first land discovered by the great navigator, although the honor has been claimed for Watling's Island. The Spaniards enslaved, outraged, robbed and murdered the Indians, until their extermination rendered further atrocities impossible.

The English occupied the islands from 1629 until 1641. An interval of Spanish misrule followed that period, until 1676, when the English resumed possession. But it was not until 1783 that they came permanently under the dominion of the British Crown.

The number of islands in the Bahama group is variously estimated at from three to four hundred. Like the Bermudas they owe their origin to the coral insect, and their upper strata of soil is made up of a concrete mass of coral and shelly sand. They extend in a curved line six hundred miles long, and in a north-westerly direction. Their western extremity is separated by the Gulf Stream from Florida, and the Bahama channel lies between the south-eastern island and Cuba. They stretch from twenty degrees to twenty-seven degrees north latitude. There are few hilly districts in the islands; most of the land is flat and scarcely raised above the level of the sea. The soil is rich and exceedingly productive. Corn, beans, and potatoes are raised in large quantities. All the tropical fruits, such as figs, oranges, bananas, grow on all the islands. Logwood, cedar and satinwood trees are also abundant.

The Bahamas are sufficiently removed from the tropics to escape the burning rays of the equatorial sun. The climate is mild and equable in winter, and warm without undue heat in summer. The winter lasts from November to April. During this period the temperature rarely runs above seventy degrees Fahr., or falls below sixty degrees Fahr. The sea breezes coming in from the north keep up a delightful temperate coolness which is exceedingly grateful to patients from New York's changeable climate. In the summer the mercury seldom reaches ninety degrees Fahr. or falls below seventy degrees. As the islands are flat, the sea breezes from all sides sweep over every part, and the atmosphere is thus changed, and kept pure and temperate. There are no indigenous diseases.

The foreign visitors, however, who come long distances in an incurable state, swell somewhat the sick-list and mortuary records. For several years past some of these islands have become resorts for the class of consumptives who thrive best in a moist atmosphere.

New Providence is the principal island of the group. It is twenty miles long, seven miles wide, and extends from east to west. Near the coast is a range of hills, upon a part of which Nassau, the capital of the group, is built.

Nassau is in latitude twenty-five degrees north. It is well laid out, has capacious streets, and is the great centre of commerce and industry in these parts. The harbor is very fine and well protected. During the Southern war it gained considerable repute as a refuge and a starting-point for blockade runners. Since their trade ceased, the city has gone back in a business point of view, and the false temporary prosperity which it then gained has already left it.

The climate is very healthy. The weather during the winter is mild, clear and invigorating. The atmosphere is usually moist, and is therefore not suited for invalids who prefer a dry air. The special needs of the patients must be determined before they leave home. If a cool, dry air is best suited for them—and this fact is easily ascertained—they must not go to Nassau. From meteorological records which we have before us, we find that the maximum temperature in January (the coldest month of the year) was eighty degrees Fahr., while the minimum was fifty-eight. In July, the warmest month, the highest point reached by the mercury was ninety degrees—the lowest eighty-three. In February the maximum temperature was seventy-eight—the lowest sixty-eight. The greatest amount of rain falls in the summer months, but there is also considerable rain in winter.

Patients should not prolong their stay into the summer months unless they have recovered their normal standard of strength, and are cured. Consumptives should select homes in the outskirts of Nassau, or in the country districts of other parts of the island.

Harbor Island is situated in latitude twenty-five degrees north, a few miles from Nassau. It is considered a desirable place for invalids, and many go there in preference to New Providence. The lack of facilities for communication with the outer world makes it less desirable as a place of residence.

Turk's Island, at the extreme south of the group, in latitude twenty-one degrees north, is also a good health resort. It is not as accessible as either of the islands previously mentioned. Running in a south-easterly direction from the Bahamas, the next group in importance is known as the Virgin Isles. They are not under the rule of one nation; the English, Spanish, and Danish governments hold various parts. There are three principal islands here, frequented by American tourists for health and pleasure; viz., Santa Cruz, St Thomas, and St. Vincent. Santa Cruz or St. Croix, as it is sometimes called, is situated in latitude eighteen degrees north, and as a sanatarium has a greater reputation than the others. It is twenty-seven miles long, and seven wide, and has an area of one hundred square miles. Its soil is fertile and the general aspect of the country is pleasing. Flat undulating lands are diversified by long ranges of high hills which rise in some places to the dignity of mountains, while handsome villages grace the sloping edges of the hills or nestle in the valleys. The principal hilly portions occupy the centre and western districts of the island. All the varieties of tropical fruit grow in rich profusion and flowers bloom continually. The island has been settled so long that it is in a high state of cultivation. The roads are over one hundred miles in extent, and are as hard and firm as those of Central Park. There are no marsh or swamp lands in Santa Cruz; everything is dry, and the inhabitants are consequently free from that plague of southern climes, malaria. The west side of the island is warmer and better protected by the hills than the east side, so that very delicate persons may select a residence in this portion without danger from gales that sometimes pass over the land. August, September, and October are the stormy months, and are sometimes called the hurricane months. Very little rain falls either in winter or summer; in fact rain is one of the principal wants of the people. At one time the ordinary toast at convivial gatherings was " more rain." This dry, warm, pure atmosphere makes the climate of Santa Cruz peculiarly agreeable to persons suffering from pulmonary complaints, rheumatism, and diseases of the kidneys; many suffering from these diseases find relief even from a short residence. A correspondent of the *Post*, who had winter experiences at different parts on the shores of the Mediterranean ports, says "that for equability of temperature, security from reverses for the invalid, a soothing balm in every breath that is drawn, with the accompaniments of natural claims, Santa Cruz has no competitor."

The thermometer ranges during the winter months from seventy-six to eighty-two degrees. In summer the heat is very slightly increased.

Comfortable homes are to be found in all parts of the island. In the principal towns, Christiansted and Frederickstadt, there are good hotels. But the villages or plantations among the hills offer the most desirable homes, both in point of comfort and healthfulness.

Santa Cruz is reached by the Brazilian line of steamers from New York to St. Thomas, and thence a sail of four hours lands the passenger in Christiansted.

St. Thomas, the second island in commercial importance belonging to this group, has also some reputation as a health resort. It is situated thirty-eight miles east of Porto Rico. The surface land is hilly and without the natural and artificial beauty of Santa Cruz. The productions of the soil, with one or two exceptions, are unprofitable. Cocoa-nut groves are plentiful, and some cotton is raised. Water is scarce, and for all household purposes the inhabitants have to depend on the rain. The principal harbor, St. Thomas, is a stopping-place for nearly all the steamships that visit the West India Islands. They maintain the prosperity of the place, and give to it its prominence as a commercial centre. The climate is very mild and equable, especially in winter. It is somewhat warmer than Santa Cruz—more tropical in character. Malarial diseases are more frequent. Invalids should avoid the night air as much as possible. Some forms of Bright's disease of the kidneys and consumption are cured by this climate. Though inferior to Santa Cruz as a sanatarium, it is worthy of a trial.

The island of St. Vincent, held by the British, is one of the most productive and interesting of the West India group. It is located in latitude thirteen degrees ten minutes north, measures eighteen miles in its longest diameter, and is eleven miles broad. It is about ninety miles from Barbadoes.

The surface land is made up of mountains and picturesque fertile valleys. The mountain chain runs from north to south, and is covered by dense forests. Souffriere, the principal volcanic mountain, is three thousand feet above the level of the sea, and has a crater three miles in circumference. The cultivated sides of the mountains are very rich, and agricultural products of all kinds are plentiful. The most unpleasant feature of the country is the enormous quantity of rain which falls yearly. In some localities it reaches over one hundred cubic inches. But the subsoil is gravelly and the flowing streams are free and numerous, so the soil does not retain the water; consequently the healthfulness of the place is not impaired. The weather during winter and summer is warm and equable. In January the lowest temperature is seventy-two degrees, the highest eighty-four; monthly mean, seventy-eight degrees. During July of the same year, the thermometer ranged between seventy-eight and eighty-seven degrees. These small variations of temperature are unusual, and show conclusively that the climate is a desirable one for that class of invalids who thrive in a warm, equal, moist atmosphere. It is not as suitable for patients with Bright's disease, as those islands where the moisture is at a minimum.

Kingston, the capital town, is on the south-west coast. It is a thriving, busy place, and considered

6

quite healthy. The high districts near this town, however, are much more desirable resting-places. The patient should be furnished with waterproof clothing and thin flannels.

Barbadoes, the most easterly of the Caribbee Islands, and one of the most important, is situated in latitude thirteen degrees four minutes north. It is twenty-two miles long, fourteen broad, and has an area of one hundred and sixty-six square miles. The Portuguese discovered it in 1600, but established no settlements. In 1605, the British planted their flag on the spot now occupied by Bridgetown, the capital of the island. The base of the island is of calcareous origin. The surface land is, for the most part, flat, with the exception of the north-eastern portion. Here there is a gradual elevation, which at some points is eleven hundred feet above the sea-level. Part of the soil is sandy and porous ; in some places there is a rich dark loam, which is very productive. The whole island is under cultivation. Its green fields, and rich groves of tamarinds and other trees, give it a fine appearance. The climate is everywhere warm, equable, and healthy. The thermometer, in

December, ranges from seventy-three to eighty-five degrees, in February from seventy-one to eighty-four degrees. The sea breezes sweep over the whole land, and keep the air pure and comparatively cool. Occasionally fierce storms occur, which do some damage to houses near the coast; otherwise there is no unpleasant weather. Consumptives and patients with Bright's disease often find this climate of great benefit, and a residence of a few months in winter is certain, in the majority of cases, to produce a change for the better, if not a perfect cure. Either at Bridgetown or Speight's Town, or in any of the villages or plantations in the country districts, good homes may be had, with all necessary accommodations.

There are many favored localities in the island of Cuba, where the health-giving properties of the climate are such as all consumptive invalids need. But at the present time its disturbed social condition renders it unfit as a residence for nervous invalids. A few words, however, respecting its climatic characteristics will not be out of place. The island is the largest and richest of the Antilles. It extends from latitude nineteen degrees fifty minutes to twenty-three degrees nine minutes north. The central portions of the island are mountainous. An extensive range, the Copper Mountains, runs through the central portion, and is covered with dense forests. The neighboring valleys and cultivated slopes are exceedingly mild and healthy. The rainy season in Cuba occurs during the summer, and the rain-fall is very large, amounting to nearly one hundred cubic inches yearly. The climate is essentially an open-air one. People eat, drink, and even sleep out-doors. Although under a tropical sun, the heat, except in extraordinary seasons, and occasionally at noon, is never very oppressive. The air is kept in motion by the cooling breezes from the sea. The best season for invalids is from the first of December until the last of March. Summer months in Cuba are decidedly unhealthy. Yellow-fever often prevails in the seaports, and mild types of remittent and intermittent fevers appear in the interior districts.

Some invalids prefer Havana and its environs as a winter residence, but there are more suitable places. Matanzas, San Antonio, Santiago, or some of the villages in the interior, near the mountains, are preferable. In the winter season Matanzas is delightfully mild. The pure sea breezes temper the sun's rays. The town is located on the south-western part of Matanzas Bay. It has the same Spanish look, and its people the same Spanish customs, that are the noticeable features in other parts of Cuba. Malarial fevers prevail to some extent in the town and low lands in the neighborhood. There is a hill called the Cumbre, back of the place upon which many private residences are built. If board can be had in any of these, the patient would find himself with the best surroundings that can be had in Cuba.

The climate of San Domingo or Hayti is highly spoken of. The dry season, from December to the latter part of March, is the best for invalids. During these months the weather is remarkably fine. The air is warm but exhilarating. As the island is mountainous, different regions present different thermal variations, and the traveller can find places cool, or very warm and sheltered. Patients suffering from disease of the kidneys, rheumatism, and pulmonary complaints, find great relief from a few months' residence. The change from the cold, raw, damp atmosphere of our Northern cities to a genial sunny home cannot but be followed by good results. There is some malaria in the flat lands of the island, but the types of disease resulting from its introduction into the system, are mild in comparison with similar fevers in the United States.

San Domingo extends from eighteen degrees to twenty-one degrees north latitude. It is four hundred miles long and one hundred and fifty wide. The principal city is San Domingo. Throughout the island there are many interesting places, where the traveller, by a judicious method of " roughing it, " may enjoy himself exceedingly.

Some of the Dutch West India Islands near Venezuela enjoy the benefits of a healthy climate. They are best suited for persons with kidney diseases. The principal island of this group—Curaçoa—has long been a favorite resort for sufferers from Bright's disease. Some also with consumption receive great benefit by a sojourn there. The principal town of this island is Willemstad. It is finely situated,

very healthy, and excellent accommodations may
be had for invalids and tourists.

There is constant communication between New
York and the various islands of the Antilles. Elegant steamers—safe and in the hands of able officers
—leave at intervals of a week for Cuba, St. Thomas,
San Domingo, Nassau in the Bahamas, and other
ports; and from them smaller vessels can always
be obtained to transport the traveller to islands of
lesser note.

## CHAPTER IX.

### BERMUDA ISLANDS.

Coraline formations—Where the zoophytes work—Composition of coral—Soil produced by coral sand and decaying vegetation—Location of islands—Trade winds—Prevailing winds—Thermal characteristics in winter and summer—Rain-fall—Prevalent diseases—Annual mortality—Best months for consumptives and other invalids—What to eat, drink, and wear—When to exercise—Bermuda, St. George, Somerset, Ireland—Towns of Hamilton and St. George.

In the warm latitudes of all parts of the globe, coraline formations lift their heads above the waters. The architect *zoophytes*, with tireless energy, by their delicate work have created "oases in the desert of waters," where the storm-driven mariner may find a refuge and a rest. They have indeed builded better than they knew in lifting up these small islands in the trackless ocean.

As the islands under consideration owe their origin to the little zoophyte, it may not be amiss to examine for a moment the peculiarities of its work. It usually commences operations thirty or forty feet below the surface of the water on some pre-existing rocky formations. This fact has been proved by careful investigations. The old idea that they began to build in the uttermost depths of the ocean is consequently no longer tenable. The polyp attaching itself to the rock, secretes a calcareous substance which is cemented and hardened by a peculiar animal matter. This gives to coral greater firmness and smoothness. The little builders themselves increase by a process of budding. Small projections grow out from the body of the parent, which live and act independently, and finally separate from the parent stem, when the latter's term of life and work is ended. And thus the work is kept up; the laborers increase with the labor to be performed. The manufacture of coral takes place with rapidity. It grows several feet in less than a year. Channels which have been cut through coral reefs deep enough to allow of the passage of large vessels, have been almost entirely filled up in the space of ten years. Some of the principal groups of islands in the Atlantic and Pacific are formed of coral. The base of the Bermudas and the reefs around are entirely of coraline

growth.    According to Nelson the surface rock
of the islands has been formed at the expense of
the projecting coral reefs.   Violent storms crum-
bled them into sand, which was carried along and
piled in drifts by the winds and waves.   Mixed with
all kinds of sea-shells, in the course of time it hardened, and now exists as a rock of creamy white color—very porous, but not liable to crumble after exposure to the air.   It makes excellent building stone
and is much employed for that purpose in the islands.   This hard surface is free from water and
dampness.   Springs of water do not exist anywhere.
No amount of boring will reach drinking water.
The inhabitants have to depend solely on the clouds
for their supply of drinking water.   The number of
the Bermudas is variously estimated.   Some with an
abnormal aptitude for counting, run the number up
to eight hundred—others make it five hundred—but
irrespective of the little jagged rocks which lift their
brown heads above the waters, the number of islands—which may with truth be termed islands—
does not exceed one hundred.   These do not extend
over twenty miles in their longest diameter, and the

width of the widest is about three quarters of a mile.
They lie in latitude 30° 20' north, and longitude 64°
50' west, and in a direct line are six hundred miles
from Cape Hatteras, North Carolina. They are seven hundred miles from New York. Twenty of
the islands are inhabited. The five largest include
Bermuda (also called the continent or mainland).
St. George's, St. David's, Somerset, and Ireland.
Bermuda and St. George's are the principal islands
visited by tourists and invalids. Like most of the
islands and continents on this hemisphere, they owe
their discovery to the enterprise of a Spaniard named
Juan Fernandez, who landed there in 1527, but the
islands were afterwards lost sight of until 1609, when
Sir George Somers was wrecked on the Isle of Devils
while on his way to a colony in Virginia. Shortly
after the Virginia Company had the islands incor-
porated in their charter, and they have remained a
dependence of Great Britain ever since. This power
has developed an industrious colony and made the island harbors a rendezvous for her men-of-war in the
Atlantic. The land is exceedingly productive. Fruits
grow and flowers bloom everywhere. The pome-

granate, fig and orange grow up with pears and fruit of more northern climes. The cocoanut, India-rubber, waving palm, and tamarind-trees, with the Pride of India, are found in all parts. Bananas are raised in large quantities.

The climate of the Bermudas has been highly extolled by tourists and invalids who have sojourned there during the winter months. The weather is mild and does not produce the languor of other atmospheres nearer the tropics. This fine weather, however, is frequently interrupted by fierce storms. The prevailing winds in winter are west and north-west. The south-west wind brings with it violent storms, and a change in the temperature of about fourteen degrees. The mean temperature of the winter months is sixty degrees Fahr., and the mercury rarely falls below forty degrees in the coldest and stormiest weather. In the summer months it is considered unusual to have the temperature remain for any length of time above eighty-five degrees F. The air is generally moist, and its warmth is kept up by the influence of the Gulf stream, which flows between the islands and the American coast. The

nights are cool.  Rain falls copiously in winter.
The rain is caught in tanks on the house-tops and in
the rocks, and stored for household purposes.  At
first sight it would seem that the prevailing moisture of the air, with heat, would not be conducive to
health, but the mortuary records exhibited by Dr.
Gidet state the average mortality at 14.5. per cent.
From the influx of visitors afflicted with consumption
and kindred complaints the death-rate of late years
has been very likely increased.  Malarial diseases
are unknown on the islands, unless among those who
have brought the disease with them.  Once in every
five or six years yellow-fever epidemics occur in the
summer.  Its ravages are often increased by the
crowded condition of the hulks and vessels in the
harbors and the bad ventilation of the ports and hospital.  Rheumatic diseases are rare, and persons suffering from rheumatism sometimes find relief by
residing a few weeks on the islands, even without
the aid of medicines.

The consumptives most benefited by the climate
are those whose disease originated in inflammation
of the bronchial tubes—*i.e.*, inflammatory or catarrhal

phthisis. The tubercular form of consumption does not experience the same degree of relief. But this may arise from the fact that the disease is associated with greater debility than the other, and the patients are therefore unable to resist the depressing influences of a long journey, and a boarding-house life among strangers. If a patient cannot walk a mile or two without much fatigue he should stay at home. Chronic bronchitis in all its forms is benefited by the climate of Bermuda.

Asthmatics are frequently benefited by a few weeks' residence in Bermuda during the winter months. If the climate is suitable for them a change for the better is noticed immediately. If they do not experience relief within the first fortnight of their sojourn, another resort should be tried. Tourists and invalids suffer considerably from indiscretions in eating and drinking during the early part of their visit. As the inhabitants are to a great extent isolated from the surrounding world, social and convivial gatherings are frequent. Late dinners and wine-drinking are fashionable. Strangers require but little urging to make them fall in with the customs of the country. They eat and drink until some inflammatory disease of the digestive organs awakens them to a sense of propriety. During the first few weeks' residence a greater regularity of diet and abstinence from alcoholic stimulus should be observed than is necessary at home. In fact such persons are better without alcohol. The poison seldom assists the cure of disease. The utmost care is necessary until the system becomes accustomed to the change of air, water, and diet. Every excess must be avoided, or the weakened frame will receive an extra blow from which it cannot recover.

Flannel must be worn next the skin from November until March. Extra clothing is specially necessary after sundown, as the nights are always cool.

The Island of Bermuda, also known as the continent or mainland, is the largest of the group. Hamilton, the principal town, is the centre of the enterprise and business of the island. Hamilton is a town of two thousand inhabitants. The houses are built of the peculiar shelly sandstone previously referred to. The roofs are plastered and fitted so as to catch the rain. The front street close to the water is shaded on each side by the beautiful Pride of India trees. The bark of this tree has some re putation as a cathartic and anthelmintic. The principal hotel is near the back part of the town. It is said to be well kept. There is a level district behind the city half a mile wide. Beyond that the country is hilly. The wealthy inhabitants of the isl- and live in handsome cottages in these suburbs or on neighboring islands; very few people live in town after business hours, and at night when the stores are closed it has a deserted appearance, no life or bustle visible anywhere.

Invalids seeking a residence in Hamilton may re- side in the hotel or some of the cottages in the wooded districts in other parts of the island. The latter are preferable. There is excellent fishing and bathing in the transparent waters around the island. The temptation to bathe too long is very great, but invalids must remember that it is dangerous. Five minutes in the water is sufficiently long for delicate persons, and from fifteen to twenty minutes is enough for the healthiest. Bathing, like all other good things, is very injurious when taken in excess.

St. George's Island is about three miles in length, and half a mile wide at its widest part. It has a fine harbor, whose waters are exceedingly clear and transparent. It is walled in on all sides, with the exception of the entrance, which is extremely narrow and protected by a fort. The town derives its name from Sir George Somers, who was wrecked here. In its appearance and surroundings it is essentially Spanish. The streets are narrow, irregular, and run hither and thither without any regard to symmetry or neatness. The suburbs and outlying portions of the island are exceedingly productive, and bloom with a rich profusion of fruit and flowers. This island was a favorite resort for privateers during the war of secession. It was there also that Dr. Blackburn and others were said to have concocted the plan of introducing yellow-fever into the cities of the Northern States. Although there are many interesting places in and around St. George, invalids prefer remaining in Bermuda. There is more life and more social enjoyment in the latter place, and the majority of

people away from home are attracted there in consequence. A circle of sympathizing acquaintances is
a preventive of homesickness (*nostalgia*), a disease
which affects visitors to islands in the middle of the
Atlantic.

Somerset Island, one of the most fertile of the
Bermudas, was named after Robert Carr, Earl of
Somerset. It has no town of importance, or harbor
suitable for trading vessels. There are many fine
residences scattered about in picturesque localities,
and those who like a good home, quiet and unosten-
tatious, will be suited there, and benefited by the
pure balmy atmosphere.

Ireland is an island used almost entirely by the
British Government for military purposes. It is
one mile long, and one and a quarter broad. One
of the largest floating docks in the world lies in the
harbor. It was towed across the ocean by five steamships. It is three hundred and eighty-seven feet in
length. The British have also established here a
hospital for their sick soldiers and employés in the
dock-yards. During epidemics it is usually over-
crowded, and the mortality is very great. With

proper ventilation, and greater accommodation for patients, the mortality would be much smaller. Between Ireland and Somerset is the small island of Boaz. It is connected by a bridge with the former place, and by a ferry with the latter. Constant communication is kept up between the various inhabited ·islands by means of boats, carriages, and bridges. The traveller is thus enabled to make many interesting excursions to the various islands of the group. If he is inclined to study the life of the myriads of molluscæ and other industrious dwellers of the coral mass and jagged rocks jutting out from the transparent waters, he can do so with great satisfaction.

The communication between the Bermuda Islands and New York is not very frequent. In the winter months vessels leave once in each fortnight. In the spring and summer, weekly trips are made.

# CHAPTER X.

## SANDWICH ISLANDS.

Location—Structure of the Islands—Thermal variations at different altitudes—-Climate of northern and southern shores —Effects of trade-winds on climate—Rain-fall in Hilo and Honolulu—Absorption of moisture by the soil—Products of civilization—Prevalent diseases—Resorts for consumptives—Peculiarities of climate in Oahu, Hawaii, Maui—Three principal towns, Honolulu, Lahaina and Hilo.

The Hawaiian or Sandwich Islands form a chain in the great watery desert of the Pacific, three hundred and sixty miles long, curved from east to west and from north to south. The northern extremity of the chain is situated at twenty-one degrees, and the southern island, Hawaii, at nineteen degrees north latitude. They are in a direct line between Canton and San Francisco. While the earth was yet in its infancy these islands were thrown up from the ocean's bed by volcanic action. Even at the present day their subterranean origin is fully shown. The mountains and valleys consist mainly of a mixture

of lava and sand, to which is added at the lower mountain slopes, a rich deposit of vegetable mould produced by ages of decay.   Immense coral reefs stretch
out from the shore in various parts, forming natural breastworks for the protection of their harbors.

Although within the tropics, the climate approx-
imates to that of the temperate zone.   The ocean
which surrounds them and the trade winds which
are constantly blowing over the land maintain an
agreeable and bracing atmosphere, which countries
in the same latitude seldom possess.   The trade
winds (or constant winds as they are sometimes
called), coming from north of the equator, blow over
the land in a north-easterly or north-westerly direction.   The northern and easterly portions of the islands receive their full force, and consequently are
often subject to disagreeable and changeable weather.
Great rains varying with fierce gales are of common occurrence.   The severity of these winds, however, is diminished by the mountains, which take
away their coldness and condense their vapor into
rain and snow before they reach the south-eastern
shores.   There is a striking difference in climate on

the two sides of these islands. On one it is constantly dry—on the other as constantly wet. In
one portion it is almost impossible to obtain sufficient water for drinking and agricultural purposes, while in another the country is full of overflowing streams, and rain-storms are frequent. Thus
in the district of Hilo, on the island of Hawaii,
there are sixty streams running down to the ocean.
At Kowa, on the other side, water has to be carried
in barrels for the ordinary uses of the inhabitants.
At Hilo it often rains steadily for three weeks,
while in the former region perhaps not more
than one day in the year. The rain-fall in Hilo
is about *seventeen feet in twelve months;* in Kowa,
forty-five inches. Yet with this vast amount of
moisture the north-eastern slopes are not unhealthy.
The lava soil is porous and the water drains off
rapidly, leaving the ground dry and fit for walking.

It is said that the islanders have no word in their
language to signify weather. Many attempt to explain this by saying that with a climate so equable
and mild there was no need of the term. It is more
likely that they could not find a term strong enough

to express the sudden and uncomfortable changes on the northern side of the whole chain of islands.

The hottest month in the year is June—the coldest is January. The thermal variations along the southern coast are small. The mean temperature of the year is stated by Dr. T. M. Coan at seventy-five degrees Fahr., and the diurnal variation in the best weather about fifteen degrees. During the northeast storms which sometimes prevail in the spring and fall months, the thermal variations often amount to thirty degrees. The climate of the southern portion of the islands, however, is an excellent one for invalids. It is mild and invigorating, and especially suitable for those suffering from consumption in its incipient stages.

Patients troubled with Bright's disease or rheumatism also receive some benefit by a residence there.

Though living in a land comparatively free from endemic diseases the native inhabitants are fast dying out. When Capt. Cook visited the islands in 1779, the population numbered between three and four hundred thousand. Ninety years later the number dwindled to fifty-six thousand. This rapid decrease is still going on, and will only end with their total annihilation. The causes of this decay are many. They owe their origin mainly to the farcical civilization of the nineteenth century and its polluted accompaniments. The people were vigorous, hardy, and prolific when the islands were first thrown open to commerce. Since then their history has been marked by disease, degradation, and death. The influx of foreign visitors from so-called Christian ports introduced and developed gambling, drinking, licentiousness, and the worst forms of specific disease. Having thus disseminated their rottenness and sin and destroyed a nation, we are now called upon to look at the beautiful results in the shape of free schools and an educated people, and shut our eyes to the rest. All the work, all the absorbing labor and energy of the devoted missionaries have not been sufficient to counterbalance the frightful evils afflicted by their own countrymen. The majority of the natives are industrious only in their licentiousness, and they lack the moral power to do better. Nothing can save them from total annihilation—not even their education, or the religion of those under the direct care and supervision of the missionaries. The principal diseases which flourish among the natives are syphilis, leprosy, and aneurism. On the island of Molokai there is a leper hospital into which all those tainted with leprosy are placed. They are clothed and fed by the government. Persons who have visited them say that they seem to be comfortable and happy in the midst of their terrible surroundings. Malarial fevers do not prevail to any extent. When they do occur they are of an exceedingly mild type. The natives, when attacked, labor under severe depression of spirits and cry and act in a childish manner; hence the disease has been named the *Boo-hoo* fever. Aneurisms and other diseases of the circulatory system are not uncommon. Some attribute them to the enervating influence of the climate, to its relaxing effect on the blood-vessels.

It is more than probable that the prevalence of venereal diseases among all classes is the real cause of these afflictions. One of the most common causes of degeneration of the arterial walls is syphilis. Whether this explanation be the correct

7

one or not, persons suffering from diseases of the circulatory apparatus should not visit the islands for
any length of time.   Consumption carries off a large
number of the native population.   Among the
foreign residents it is rare.

The atmosphere of the southern portions of these
islands being free from dampness and very mild,
sufferers from pulmonary complaints are benefited
by it.   Invalids can live in the open air ; taking exercise and enjoying the sunshine during the winter
months without inconvenience or harm.   The occasional occurrence of a " north-easter " is of no consequence ; it rather helps to relieve the monotony of a
long period of fine weather.

The islands principally resorted to by invalids
are Oahu, Maui, and Hawaii.   There are nine other
islands in the group, but none of them have places
suitable for the accommodation of strangers.

The island of Oahu, the fourth in size and the.
first in importance, contains the principal towns and
harbor of the entire group.   The city of Honolulu
is situated on its south-east side, on the borders of
the harbor of the same name.   It has a population

of about fifteen thousand, composed principally of
foreign merchants. Beyond the town, and between
it and the mountains, lies the fertile valley of Nu-
mar. The climate of Honolulu, like other parts, is
mild throughout the year and without the tropical
heat which one would expect from its location.
There is little difference between its summer and
winter months. The warmest days in summer do
not exceed the warmest days in winter by eight
degrees. During a period of twelve years the highest point touched by the thermometer was ninety
degrees Fahr., the lowest fifty-three degrees. The
hottest mean day was seventy-five degrees, and the
coldest mean day, fifty-five. The rain-fall averages
about forty-one inches. Consumptives can live in
Honolulu all the year. They generally remain, however, only during the interval between October and
May. Invalids who suffer much from depression of
spirits, or who do not observe a change for the better within two or three weeks, had better try some
other atmosphere. They may either leave the islands
altogether, or go further up towards the mountains
where the air is cooler and more bracing. Consump-

tives who are far advanced in the disease must not
take up a residence in Honolulu. The means of communication with other parts are so limited that the
patient feels cut off from all home connection, and
as a consequence becomes depressed and receives
little benefit from the change.

There is a large, well-kept hotel in the town,
managed by the Hawaiian government, where every
reasonable comfort and accommodation can be had
at average prices. It is best, however, in all cases to
obtain if possible a residence in the suburbs. The
air is clear and pure, and more bracing. A mile
or two from town, in the Nuanu valley, are some
very pleasant villas where good board can be had
at moderate rates. The general directions regard-
ing exercise, diet, medicine, etc., given in former
chapters, is applicable here.

Maui is the second island of the group. Mauna
Halekeala, the largest volcano in the world, is situated on this island. The crater measures ninety-five
miles in circumference, and is two thousand feet
deep.

Lahaina, the principal town, lies on the south-

western side of the island.    It is protected, like Honolulu, from the violent trade-winds and rain-storms
by the mountains, and is the only place in the district suited to invalids.    The climate is somewhat
milder than at Honolulu.    The thermal variations are
about the same.    During the hottest day of 1873, the
thermometer registered eighty-six, and on the coldest day fifty-four degrees Fahr.    A short distance
above Lahaina, at an elevation of three thousand
feet above the level of the sea, the temperature was
between forty and seventy-six degrees.    The yearly
rain-fall is about thirty-nine inches.    The influx of
foreign visitors to Lahaina is not so great as at Honolulu.    The home communications are not made as
regularly; therefore it is not so desirable as a place
of residence.

Hilo, on the Island of Hawaii, is on the side exposed to the wind and rain.    It is two degrees further south than Honolulu.    The amount of rain-fall
has been previously stated at seventeen feet yearly.
Nevertheless, the town is quite healthy, and a few
invalids seem to find in its moist atmosphere something they need, and come away benefited.    Those

who need moisture in the air can get it here without stint.

The voyage from San Francisco to Honolulu consumes fourteen days. Two trips a month are made by the elegant steamers of the Pacific Mail Steamship Company. The accommodations for travellers are excellent. From Honolulu, the traveller is carried to Lahaina by schooner. The trip is made once in each week. The voyage to Hilo is made in the same manner.

# CHAPTER XI.

## COLD CLIMATES FOR CONSUMPTIVES.

What class of consumptives require a cold climate—Comparative effects of a warm and cold atmosphere—Care to be observed in the selection of suitable cases for treatment in cold
climate—Danger of living in-doors—Minnesota as a sanatarium—Exaggerated accounts of its healthfulness—Topography of the State—Variations of temperature at different
seasons—Rain-fall—Mortality among consumptives—Ratio of
recoveries—St. Paul—St. Anthony—Minneapolis—Winona—
Wabasha—Red Wing—Hutchinson—Ramapo Valley.

THE first requirement of a consumptive patient
is a residence in a dry equable climate.   And if this
can be obtained in connection with a warm atmosphere, which will enable the patient to spend much
of his time in the open air, take exercise and enjoy
the bright sunshine, nothing more can be desired.
Such climates suit the majority of persons suffering
from pulmonary complaints.   The warm air soothes
the sensitive lining membrane of the diseased air-
passages, relaxes the skin and keeps it in healthy
action, so that it is enabled to relieve the lungs of

part of its work of throwing out of the system the products of decay, at the same time diminishing the temperature of the body by increasing the perspiration. With regard to the latter, we are not referring to sufferers so far advanced in disease as to be weakened by hectic night-sweats.

There are some few consumptives on whom a warm atmosphere exerts a debilitating effect. Such persons find no life, no vitality in the air, and languor and lassitude, increasing with their stay, soon destroy all chance of recovery. For this class a cold climate is especially suitable. The cold bracing air, containing as it does more oxygen in a given space than the lighter and warmer air, gives their lungs the food which they need to stay the inroads of the disease. But the temperature of the place selected must not be so continuously low as to prevent the patient from remaining out-of-doors several hours during the day. If invalids cannot go out they lose all the benefit of the stimulating air. It is, therefore, of considerable importance that the residence selected shall not be so cold as to prevent out-door exercise. The consumptives who improve in a cold climate are those who feel better on cold clear days and uncomfortable on warm ones. Usually these persons are of a nervous-sanguine temperament, easily depressed and as readily excited.

Only those in the incipient stages of consumption should seek a residence in northern regions as a means of cure. A certain amount of bodily vigor is necessary to allow of out-door exercise with the mercury at zero; then riding, walking, or working in the pure bracing air is followed by general stimulation of the circulation. This tends to remove the congestion in or near the tubercular deposits in the lungs, increases the appetite, and restores the patient to health. There is nothing better than a good circulation to diminish or prevent tubercular deposit in the lungs. There are several Northern States steadily cold in winter, which enjoy a certain repute as resorts .for consumptives. Among them may be mentioned Minnesota, the Adirondack Mountains, the mountainous regions of New Hampshire, Hampton, Long Island, and Suffern's, in Rockland county, New York. Minnesota especially has occupied a prominent position in this connection. Her praises

7*

have been long and loudly sung. Facts have been mingled with the fancies of interested writers, and truthful reports of its healthfulness hidden by exag gerations to such an extent as to make it somewhat difficult to sift the elements of truth from the mass of error. For instance, in that wonderful climate we read of *robust* individuals *with only one lung*, doing the work of a man with two, and looking fully as well, and of persons in the last stages of con sumption, with scarcely any lungs at all, completely recovering. In order to arrive at correct conclu sions in this matter, let us briefly glance at the topo graphy and climatic peculiarities of this State.

Minnesota is located at a central point of this con tinent. It is bounded on the north by British America, and on the south by Iowa, on the east by Lake Superior and Wisconsin, and on the west is the territory of Dakota. The State occupies about the same latitude as Maine, extending from forty-three degrees to forty-nine degrees north lati tude. Although a comparatively level country, it has an elevation above the sea of one thousand feet. In the north-western portion, which contains the high-

lands, there is a further rise of four hundred and
fifty feet. The land is covered with thick forests of
pine and spruce. The temperature is five or six degrees lower than in other parts of the State. Lower
down, in the valley of the Red River, is a rich allu-
vial soil composed of a dark mould. The Mississippi
Valley region, extending over seven hundred miles
through the State, is the most productive. It is the
garden of the State and the part most frequently
visited by invalids. The central and inland location of Minnesota protects it to a great extent from
the sudden and violent changes of the States on the
eastern coast. There is very little moisture in the
air and rain for the same reason. The winters are
long and exceedingly cold. The average winter
lasts one hundred and forty days, during which time
the mean temperature is sixteen degrees below the
freezing-point of water. This intense and continu-
ous cold is, however, not uncomfortable. It is
steadily cold and dry, without diurnal variations of
importance, and in this respect is relieved of one of
the disagreeable features of our eastern Atlantic
climate. The mean spring temperature is forty-five

degrees, in autumn it varies from forty-five **to** forty-six degrees. The mean annual temperature is about forty-four degrees. In the summer the mercury averages seventy degrees—a difference between winter and summer of fifty-four degrees. This great variation might at first sight seem incompatible with an equable climate, but it must be remembered that this is a *yearly* variation, and that the diurnal variations are very small. The summer heat of Minnesota is as great as it is in New Jersey. It is six or seven degrees hotter than in Utica.* The cold in winter and the heat in summer is subject to but little variation, and the sudden changes, so injurious to persons in delicate health, are almost entirely absent.

The rain-fall amounts to about twenty-five cubic inches yearly. In New England it is estimated at fifty-three inches.

It will be seen by the above that the climate of Minnesota is extremely cold in winter and warm in summer, and that the general condition of the atmos-

---

* Bill on Climate of Minnesota.

phere is dry and bracing. All these elements go far
towards making a healthy climate. The next point
to be considered is, is it a good winter resort for
consumptives? Bill and other writers speak of it
as being an incomparable sanatarium for those suffering from pulmonary complaints, and they furnish
statistics to prove their statements. Figures may
speak the truth or they may misrepresent, and in
this case the figures of comparative mortality furnished by a certain author do mislead. He com-
pares the mortuary records of States which are noted
for the prevalence of consumption with his own State,
and then draws the inference that Minnesota is the
best residence for a consumptive in the Union.
Thus, he gives the rate of mortality in Massachusetts
from consumption as one in two hundred and fifty-
four; in New York, one in four hundred and seventy-three; in Virginia, one in seven hundred and
fifty-seven; and in Minnesota, one in eleven hundred
and thirty-nine. But he fails to state that in Georgia the percentage of deaths from consumption is
not half as great as it is in the latter State. Such
one-sided reports do harm, because they are apt to

cause numbers of invalids, irrespective of case or condition, to go to this and other resorts to die. It has been estimated that of all those who visit Minnesota with consumption only one in fifteen recover. And it is also well known that the St. Paul's Young Men's Christian Association is put to great trouble and expense in burying unfortunate strangers, who arrived there merely to die, induced, possibly, by some of the glowing reports previously referred to, to quit the comforts of home when utterly unable to do without them. The cold, clear air of the State is undoubtedly beneficial to certain cases of consumption. None, however, should attempt the journey whose lungs are seriously diseased, or who have not the strength to take daily exercise in the open air. It is the open-air life after all that does the work of curing, and it is therefore little less than suicide for invalids to seek a home where they are compelled to shut themselves in-doors day after day.

Having selected a residence suited to the patient's taste, the next care should be his clothing and food. Extra flannels should be worn. In some cases a chamois-leather shirt or vest worn during the day is needed to afford complete protection to the chest. Thick, solid, waterproof boots or moccasins, worn over several pairs of stockings, are necessary to keep out the cold and damp. If the feet are kept warm and dry, and the chest protected, there is little or no danger of taking cold. While out-of-doors in cold weather it is always well to keep the mouth closed, and to breathe through the nose. The cold air is thus modified before it reaches the bronchial tube and air-cells, and is less likely to produce irritating coughing spells. Large moustaches also afford some protection to the air-passages, and their growth should be cultivated both in warm and cold climates.

St. Paul is one of the principal health resorts in Minnesota. It is extensively patronized by consumptive invalids. The city was formerly designated by the classical title of "Pig's Eye." Early in 1680, the first European, Hennipen, a Franciscan monk, halted his band of explorers on the ground now covered by St. Paul; but it received little attention from foreigners until the present century. Within the past fifteen years its main growth has taken place. The city is located on a commanding bluff, at the head of the navigation on the Mississippi River. It is two thousand and eighty-two miles from the mouth of this great estuary, and is one hundred feet above the level of the water. Its present site was sold in 1839 for thirty dollars by Pierre Pont, a French Canadian. The streets are arranged symmetrically, and are lined with elegant private residences and stores. As the capital of the County and State, and the centre of a vast mercantile trade, it is likely to keep on on its rapid and prosperous career. Around the city, on three sides, are high green hills, on which are many elegant private residences. In the summer months the invalid should seek a home in the suburbs, as it is much cooler there than in the city. When the cold weather sets in, a residence in the city is the best. Excellent hotels and equally good boarding-houses are to be found everywhere. Within a distance of three or four miles from St. Paul are several beautiful lakes, much resorted to by sportsmen and invalids during the summer.

Some tourists prefer Minneapolis and its vicinity as a temporary residence. The town is the capital

of Hennepin county, and is located on the west
bank of the Mississippi.  It is in a healthy location;
the air is dry, cold, and invigorating.  It is not protected, however, as much as the city of St. Paul, and
consequently not so desirable for a residence.

The town of St. Anthony, ten miles from St. Paul,
is situated near the falls of the same name.  It is
built on a high terrace, close to and overlooking the
falls.  There are good accommodations in boarding-
houses and hotels for travellers or invalids.

Winona is a large town, 105 miles below St.
Paul, located on the bank of the river.  It does not
lie on high ground, but is close to the margin of the
river.  The place has some reputation as a resort
for invalids.

Red Wing, higher up, is in a picturesque situation,
thoroughly sheltered by the hills.  It is a good summer resort for invalids; and for those who do not
mind being to a great extent cut off from daily communication with neighboring States, is a good winter
residence.

Sixty miles west of St. Paul there is a charming
village called Hutchinson, which as yet is not

much visited by invalids, though possessing in an
eminent degree all the sanitary advantages of a
health resort in a cold climate.  It is in one of the
healthiest districts in the State.  It is located in the
Hassan Valley, near the Hassan River, and is protected by hills which are covered with dense forests
of spruce, butternut, pine and oak.  The village is increasing rapidly in importance.  Much of its prosperity is due to the enterprise of its founders, members of the well-known Hutchinson family.

The air of the place is dry and bracing.  In winter it is steadily cold, but owing to the protected
situation of the district it is somewhat warmer than
other parts of the State.

It is not generally known that we have in the
State of New York a sanatarium for invalids
which is not excelled by any of the health resorts of
Minnesota.  Thirty miles from this city, on the Erie
Railroad, there is a pleasant village called Suffern's,
picturesquely situated in the Ramapo Valley, at the
base of the Ramapo Mountains.  It is protected on
the north, west and east by the mountains.  During
the winter the air is cold, clear and bracing, and the

thermal variations are small. Snow covers the ground from ten to twelve weeks in the season. The average temperature of winter is about forty degrees Owing to its southern exposure and protection from the north-easterly winds afforded by the mountains, the weather is never unpleasantly cold, and invalids who are in the early stages of consumption, or those suffering from chronic bronchitis, can exercise in the open air nearly every day. Miasmatic fevers are unknown in this portion of the valley. The view from Union Hill and the mountains on the north, up and down the valley, is unsurpassed. Invalids in this State, who prefer a cold climate, will do well to try the neighborhood of Suffern's before attempting the long and tedious journey to Minnesota.

# CHAPTER XII.

### HEALTH RESORTS ON THE MEDITERRANEAN.

The great inland sea—Peculiarities of temperature—Composition, tides, etc.—Northern and southern shores—Prevalent winds in winter and summer—Eastern and Western Riviera—Difference in climate between the two portions—Protection afforded by the mountains—The mistral and its effects on invalids  The sirocco, and its disease-laden breath—Prevalent diseases north and south—Dryness of the atmosphere—The Italian sun—Climate of Nice—Sudden thermal variations—Unhealthy conditions of old parts of the city—The time to visit Nice—Woollen clothing—Food and exercise—Monaco—Mentone—San Remo—Corsica, etc.

EAST of the Apennines and the Maritime Alps there are but few safe resting-places for the invalid. The cold winds come down from Northern Europe and chill the otherwise warm atmosphere. The swollen torrents and overflowing rivers inundate the valley regions during the fall and early part of winter. When the waters disappear they leave the rich decaying vegetation to breed miasmatic poison with the help of the Italian sun. Thus there is no security for the traveller, be he sick or well, in the greater part of the Central Valley region. The exceptional localities are close to the mountain wall which divides Switzerland from Italy, and will be referred to hereafter.

To the westward of the Maritime Alps, on the shores of the Mediterranean Sea, there is a brighter, milder and more genial atmosphere, a dryer and more healthful climate. The Mediterranean is the most important inland sea in the world. It is enclosed by portions of Europe, Asia, and Africa, and is connected with the Atlantic Ocean by the Straits of Gibraltar. It is warmer (fifty-four degrees F.), of a higher specific gravity, and contains more salt than the Atlantic. Its depth near the shore in many places is very great; near Nice it is about five thousand feet deep. No sea is so full of historical interest. Every wave that breaks against its mountain-fringed shore, if it could but speak, would tell many a weird tale of horror, of days when the rest of the world was in its infancy. Its history goes back to the misty mythological days when the gods condescended to make this earth the scene of their loves and hates. The descriptions of the old historians show that the northern shores of the Mediterranean possessed certain peculiarities of soil and climate which made them famous for their productiveness and healthfulness. And to this day these essential features are unchanged.

The prevailing winds of this region, from May until February, "blow from the west around northwards to north-east." * In February, March and April south-west winds prevail. According to some observers the prevailing wind in winter is from the north. The south-east wind, or *sirocco*, travels from the African deserts, and reaches the southern shores of Italy still hot and loaded with the moisture which it has collected from the Mediterranean, breeding in that region pernicious fevers, and increasing the fatality of ordinary complaints. The northern shores are happily free from this pest. Enough of its heat and moisture is stolen by the south of Italy and the mountains of Corsica † to make it cool and pleasant by the time it strikes the Riviera. This is the region to which we have to

---

* Smyth.          † Dr. Henry Bennet.

give special consideration. The Riviera or coast-line from Nice to Genoa is divided into two portions, viz., the Eastern or Riviera de Levante, and the Western or Riviera di Ponente. Western Riviera is considered the healthiest, although the whole of this region possesses a remarkably fine climate. The cold north-east winds are turned aside by the Maritime Alps, which extend from Nice to Genoa. Thus thoroughly sheltered, occupying a comparatively dry portion of the earth's surface, and open to the warm but stimulating south-west breezes of the Mediterranean, it has all the requisites of a healthy climate. The sun shines during the winter months with tropical warmth, but as the cool dry air favors evaporation from the surface, and as the air is constantly in motion, there is no oppressiveness, no debilitating influence from its rays. It is always cool in the shade and at night; in many places it is so cold that extra clothing is required. Close to the sea, it may be said to be always cool when the air is in motion. Malarial fevers are exceedingly rare in the villages and country districts along the coast. Intestinal dis-

orders prevail among strangers who come too early
in the fall, or who indulge too freely in wine and
fruit. It is the common experience of visitors
who are not extremely careful. The piercing *mistral,* or north-east wind, is much dreaded in the fall
and sometimes in the winter months. It blows from
one to four days furiously, changing the bright warm
sunshiny days to the raw, cold and damp days of a
New York March. Strangers who happen to arrive
during the prevalence of the *mistral* lose faith in
the tales they have read and heard of the beautiful
southern climate; they are apt to consider it a phan-
tasy and a dream. But if they can only develop
sufficient patience to remain until the "blow is
over," the bright warm sun will reassure them.

Nice, one of the most important resorts on the
south coast of France, is peculiarly liable to attacks
from the *mistral.* They occur generally in the
fall, and are dreaded by every invalid visitor. This
city dates back to the fifth century before Christ.
It is in about the same latitude as Portland, Maine.
The city is built on both sides of the River Paglion,
and lies between the mountains and the sea. The

mountains are on its north side and curve somewhat
towards the shore on its east and west sides. The
city is divided into two portions, the old and the new.
Visitors take up their abode in the latter quarter,
which is handsomely laid out and has wide streets
lined by fine buildings. Nearly all parts of the old
town partake of the special features of old, badly-built
towns in general, having the same amount of putrid
odors in the atmosphere, and filth in the streets. It
is decidedly unhealthy. These evils, however, work
their own cure sometimes, either by developing
epidemic diseases, or touching the pockets of house-
holders by repelling visitors from their doors. In
many respects the climate of Nice is a desirable one
for a certain class of invalids. Pulmonary consumption, either of the inflammatory or tubercular
variety in its first stages, is often completely cured
by a winter's residence there. Bronchitis, chronic
inflammations of the larynx, and catarrh of the nasal
passages are also benefited by the genial climate.
However, the invalid must not expect to have all sunshine. Rainy and stormy days occur which are decidedly harmful. A patient of ours, who resided

8

six months in Nice, informs us that on account of the cold winds, it is customary for invalids to remain in-doors after four o'clock in the afternoon. The night air is not good, being often cold and raw, and it is not unusual for the thermometer to mark a change of twenty degrees between the temperature of the day and night, and the ordinary difference between the day and night through the winter is fifteen degrees. The highest temperature in July and August, for fifteen years, was eighty-eight and a half; the lowest temperature was twenty-seven and a half F. The mean temperature for the same period was sixty and a half. The mean temperature of the month of January, 1872, was forty-seven degrees, while in February it was forty-six degrees. In July of the same year the mean temperature was seventy-five degrees. In December and January the temperature of the day varies between fifty-five and sixty-five degrees F. There are sixty rainy days in the year at Nice, but the yearly amount of rain-fall rarely exceeds thirty inches. Only a part of each of the days mentioned is wet. The rain falls for an hour or two and then the sun comes out as bright as ever and in a short time removes the moisture from the ground.

Patients intending to visit Nice should not go there before the middle of November. They will thus avoid the fall *mistral* and fall rains. Woollen clothing must be worn all winter, and at night a considerable amount of extra clothing is needed. Those with pulmonary complaints will do well to remain in-doors after sun-down in order to avoid the danger of catching cold. Exercise in the open air may be commenced about ten o'clock in the morning by weak invalids, others may commence earlier. Too much exertion at first must be avoided; in fact excess in eating, drinking, and in every good thing must be persistently avoided.

Although Nice is a suitable winter residence for some people, there are other places on the Riviera more suitable for consumptives and the weaker class of invalids. These will be described further on.

In the selection of rooms either in a boarding-house or hotel, the south side of the building in all cases is to be preferred. Rooms on the north side of the house are usually five or six degrees cooler, and in winter it is sometimes necessary to have them heated artificially.

The liliputian empire of Monaco—the smallest principality in the world—is the only resort of importance between Nice and Mentone. Lately its inhabitants rose in rebellion against its hereditary prince, for some curtailment of their rights, and drove him out of the country. But he has since returned and once more wields the sceptre. The town of Monaco dates its existence from the fourth century. It is said to derive its name from a pagan priest named Monacchus, who was placed in charge of a temple which had been built in commemoration of a great victory over the Ligurians. The remains of the temple are yet pointed out. The climate is similar to that of Nice. There are good facilities for bathing or boating; one of the principal attractions, however, is the gambling hell, which is patronized by people of all nations. During the winter the hotels and boarding-houses are filled by permanent as well as transient visitors.

Mentone, a small town of five thousand inhabitants, situated on a beautiful sheltered bay, fifteen miles from Nice, is probably the best place on the Riviera for a winter's residence. Two mountain ranges curve around it, leaving an opening to the south. Ample protection from the cold north-east and northerly winds is thus afforded. The mountain Turbia, which separates Nice from Mentone, protects the latter from the fierce mistral. These mountains are made up mainly of stratified limestone. This rock becomes gradually disintegrated and mixed with the decayed animal and vegetable matter, producing a very fertile soil. Lemon, olive and orange groves cover the mountain slopes. The lemon under the glowing Italian sun produces four crops yearly—its productiveness only ceasing with its death. On the higher ridges of the mountains pines grow in abundance. Flowers of every description bloom throughout the year. The rainy season occurs during the spring and fall months. The number of rainy days in the year is about eighty. These include every day upon which a shower occurred. But the yearly rain-fall rarely exceeds twenty-eight inches. In the summer-time rainy days are exceedingly few. Notwithstanding the fact that the wet weather occurs between October and May, the prevailing feature of the atmosphere at Mentone is dryness,* except when the south-west wind is blowing. The absence of moisture in the air is indicated by the deep blue of the sky as well as by the hygrometer. In winter the sea breezes spring up after ten in the morning, and they continue until four in the afternoon. The prevailing winds of winter are northerly. From meteorological records we find that the maximum mean temperature of the winter months, for a period of ten years, was fifty-eight degrees, and the minimum mean forty-five degrees. The lowest temperature reached during the same period was thirty-two degrees, the highest sixty-five degrees F. In August of the same year the mercury reached eighty-nine degrees, an unusual degree of heat for Mentone. At night there is a change of at least ten or twelve degrees from the temperature of the day. Frosts sometimes occur. Taking the general features of the climate at Mentone, it can be readily seen that it is well suited to invalids with incipient

* Dr. Henry Bennet's " Climate of the Mediterranean."

consumption and other affections of the pulmonary organs. And the experience of Dr. Bennet and many others adds corroborative evidence to the favorable meteorological records.

The best part of the year to spend at Mentone is between the latter part of November and March. Earlier or later than these periods, there are disagreeable objects to encounter in the shape of gnats and mosquitoes, and extremely unpleasant, changeable weather. December, January and February are generally comfortably warm and pleasant. Invalids should exercise the same precautions in the selection of a residence here that they do elsewhere. Woollen clothing is essential all winter; light flannels must be worn constantly.

Mentone and its neighborhood is entirely free from miasmatic diseases. Remittent and intermittent fevers are only seen when brought there by strangers. The climate seems to agree with visitors better than it does with those born and brought up in the town. Diseases of the air-passages, such as bronchitis, pneumonia, and consumption, are of frequent occurrence among the lower classes.

San Remo, fifteen miles from Mentone, is another winter resort of growing repute. The town, which is old and not too clean, contains about eleven thousand inhabitants. The suburbs are more suitable for invalids than the town. The thermal variations are about the same as at Mentone.

Dr. Henry Bennet, of Mentone, who has made a life study of the climates on the Mediterranean, attaches some importance to certain portions of the Island of Corsica, as resorts for consumptive invalids during the winter months. This famous island extends from forty-one degrees to forty-three degrees north latitude. It is one hundred and twenty miles long and forty-five wide. Its eastern coast is fifty miles from the Italian shores—the coast of France on the north is ninety miles distant. The island is mountainous in character. Two grand ranges run from north to south, occupying the central portions and extending in many places their rocky arms out on each side down to the sea. The eastern range of mountains is of calcareous formation. The western is made up principally of granite. This peculiarity of structure has considerable influence on the character of the soil and climate on the two sides of the island. The disintegration of calcareous rock, caused by the constant washing of the mountain streams for centuries past, has carried large quantities of the débris of these rocks, mixed with decayed animal and vegetable matter, to the coast. The constantly accumulating mass gradually dammed up many of the streams and formed large pools and lakes, which continually overflow. Along this region the soil is damp, the vegetation very rich, and under a hot Mediterranean sun miasmatic poisons are developed which make the east side an unpleasant dwelling-place. There is scarcely a spot which can be deemed healthy. The western coast is noted for its healthfulness. The granite rocks, slow to crumble, afford no such material to obstruct the watercourses. All the mountain streams have free access to the sea. Along the coast the soil is rich, but little miasm is developed. Some pleasant villages nestle in among picturesque nooks on these western slopes. Magnificent forests of the chestnut, pine, and oak cover the mountain sides. Olives, lemons, and oranges

8*

grow in rich profusion.   Cereals are also produced
in large quantities.

The principal town of the west side is Ajaccio,
the birthplace of Napoleon the First.   It is thoroughly sheltered by the mountains, and its climate
is exceedingly equable and mild during the winter
months.   Even in summer it is not too warm.   The
air contains more moisture than it does at Mentone
and other places on the Riviera.   In winter the weather is five or six degrees warmer than at Nice.   In
January the mercury varies from fifty-five to sixty
degrees during the day, and from forty to forty-four
at night.   In August the mean temperature is seventy-eight degrees.   The yearly mean temperature
is sixty-three degrees.   At night it is much warmer
than at Mentone.   The rain-fall in twelve months is
about twenty-five inches.

The best months to visit Corsica are December,
January, and February.   Malarial fevers need not
then be dreaded.

About two thousand feet above the level of the
sea, in a sheltered spot in the mountains, is a health
resort named Orezza.   The principal attractions are

the mineral springs, the waters of which are much used throughout Europe. Some of the springs have a tonic action—others are alterative. Taken in combination with the invigorating air of the place, they produce good results.

# CHAPTER XIII.

## THE MEDITERRANEAN—(CONTINUED.)

Southern shores—Varieties of climate—Moisture in the atmosphere—Misnamed health resorts—Malarial disorders—Thermal variations—Sudden changes in temperature—The sirocco—Rain-fall—Location of Pisa—Not the place for invalids at
any season of the year—Naples—Difference in climate of east
and west side—Sicily—Its physical geography and climate—
Principal towns—Products of the soil—Malaga—Algiers—Alicante.

THE southern shore of the Mediterranean is much
inferior to the northern coast as a health resort; in
fact it is decidedly unhealthy nine months in the
year. It is true there are one or two places where
the peculiarly moist climate seems to suit certain invalids; but the majority of sick travellers will do
well to remain in the north. In the latter part of
December, January, and a portion of February, it is
comparatively free from fevers, and the weather is
warm and agreeable. A residence during these
months in some of the coast towns is sometimes of

benefit to persons suffering from Bright's disease of the kidneys, and chronic pulmonary complaints of an irritating nature. Nevertheless we would not recommend an invalid to visit any of the towns in the south of Italy. The benefits are not commensurate with the risk. Inflammations of the intestinal canal, and malarial fevers of a malignant type, carry off a great many unfortunate strangers. Much of the sickness is, no doubt, due to irregularities and excesses in eating, drinking, and sight-seeing. The utter disregard of every hygienic rule, displayed by American travellers, no doubt invites disease ; but yet this will not account for the fact that a greater number of travellers die in Italy than in any other part of Europe. A list of those who annually die from what is usually known as Roman fever would startle people as well as convince them that there are more suitable dwelling-places for the sick than the south of Italy. In a visit we made in the winter of 1872, we became firmly convinced of the unhealthiness of a southern Italian climate. The whole valley region between Bologna and Rome was under water for several weeks. To reach Florence from

Pistoria, a distance of twenty miles, we were compelled to go round by way of Pisa, because the roads were destroyed by the floods.   For nearly ten weeks the ground for hundreds of miles was covered with water; and this was not an unusual occurrence. The year before, a similar inundation had taken place.  In 1873 a partial flooding of the same region was followed by a large increase in the mortality from malarial diseases.   Even under the most favorable conditions the rich vegetation of this fertile and extensive plain develops miasm.   This miasm is increased tenfold by the flood and the consequent decay of rank vegetable matter.

Sicily, and some of the towns on the coast of Spain, are not afflicted to the same degree with low types of fever.   They are, however, far behind the Riviera in point of healthfulness.   Pisa is highly spoken of by Madden and others as a winter residence for persons with pulmonary complaints, attended with much irritation of the mucous lining of the air-passages.   They say the atmosphere has strong sedative qualities, which cannot but be beneficial to the class of invalids mentioned.

nothing, however, either in its location, which is low, or in its atmosphere, which could be distorted into anything conducive to health. The town is built on both sides of the muddy Arno ; flat, marshy tracts lie between it and the sea, and the breezes coming over these tracts, loaded with moisture and miasm, are decidedly injurious.

Naples is also erroneously considered a good winter home for consumptive invalids. Perhaps for about two months in the year the climate is sufficiently free from zymotic poison to enable a stranger to get some benefit from its warm sky. A visit in the latter part of December and January is said to be always safe. The city is built on the margin of a beautiful bay. On the western side, which is not sheltered, it is often cold and disagreeable. The east side is warmed by the southerly winds, and is better suited for invalids. The mean annual temperature is sixty-two degrees. In winter the mean temperature is forty-eight degrees, and in summer it is seventy. South-west winds bring gales and cloudy weather. The south wind, or sirocco, brings a " furnace blast," and stirs up the latent disease

We saw germs in the atmosphere. A clear sky and mild, balmy days always accompany an east wind.

The sudden changes which occur in the climate of Naples show their evil effects among the native population, by developing numerous cases of pneumonia and pleurisy. The following extract from the diary of an invalid affords a good illustration of the special evils of the Neapolitan climate : *

"Feb. 18. Oh, this land of zephyrs! Yesterday it was as warm as July, to-day we are shivering with a black easterly wind, and an English black frost. I find we are come to Naples too soon. It would have been quite time enough three months hence. Naples is one of the worst climates in Europe for complaints of the chest, and the winter is much colder here than in Rome, notwithstanding the latitude. Whatever we may think of the sea-air in England, the effect is very different here. The sea-breeze in December is mild and soft ; here it is keen and piercing, and as it sets in regularly at

---

* Madden on Climate.

noon, I doubt whether Naples can be oppressively hot, even in summer.

"Feb. 14. *Ægri somnia*—if a man be tired of the slow, lingering progress of consumption, let him repair to Naples and the denouement will be much more rapid."

The Island of Sicily affords some places which are warm and salubrious in the winter months. Many cases of Bright's disease of the kidneys, bronchitis, and asthma find great relief in this climate.

Sicily is the largest island of the Mediterranean, and has a history as ancient as any in the world. It extends from thirty-six degrees to thirty-eight degrees north latitude. Originally forming part of the mainland, and separated from it by some great convulsion, it presents the same physical and geological conformation. A rugged chain of mountains occupies the centre and some portions of the coast. Etna, one of the largest volcanic mountains in the world, is on this island and directly opposite Mount Vesuvius. It is supposed that these volcanoes communicate by subterranean passages.

The climatic changes are somewhat similar to those in Southern Italy. The mean annual temperature is sixty-two degrees. The lowest point reached by the mercury is thirty-two, and the highest, when the sirocco or south-east wind blows in full force, is ninety-five degrees. There are one hundred and thirty rainy days in the year, but the annual rainfall is only twenty-five inches. Cicero said of the climate: "There is no day in the year when the sun is not visible at one time or another." Northerly and westerly winds prevail most of the year. The sirocco on its occasional visits makes every one uncomfortable by the intense heat which accompanies it, and the clouds of fine dust filled with animalculæ which it forces through everything. The sirocco makes a change in the temperature of twenty-five or thirty degrees. The climate might be characterized as moist, warm and sedative in its effects, and likely to exert a good effect on that class of invalids who breathe better in such an atmosphere. Palermo is the favorite resort on the island for invalids.

Consumptives who wish to find an exceedingly

*dry* winter climate will be suited at Malaga. This is a large seaport town on the south-east coast of Spain. It is two hundred and fifty miles south of Naples and ninety miles from the African coast. Although possessing the dryest climate on our list with the exception of Egypt, it has its disadvantages. There are two winds which are the dread of all invalids, viz. the *levanter* or east wind, and the *terral* or north-west wind. In summer the former gives a pleasant coolness to the atmosphere, but in the winter it is excessively cold and accompanied by rain, and does infinite damage to weak and irritable invalids. The terral is hot in summer, but very cold in winter, and it carries with it clouds of fine sand which produces great irritation of the cutaneous surface. The prevailing winds are northerly. January is the coldest and February the hottest month in the year. Diseases are more fatal in January than in any other month. Consumption is not uncommon among the native population of Malaga. Deaths occur annually from that disease in the proportion of thirty-four in one thousand. Many cases of pleurisy and pneumonia occur when the *terral* has ceased blowing. Strangers are sometimes afflicted with a peculiar inflammatory affection of the gums, said to arise from the acid wine of the country. It commences with a purplish swelling at the margin of the gums, which is soon followed by ulceration. The disease is easily cured.

During December, January, and February the thermometer in the shade ranges from sixty to sixty-four degrees, and from eighty-five to ninety in the summer. The mean temperature of January is fifty-eight degrees F.; mean annual temperature is sixty-five degrees, four degrees lower than in Jacksonville, Florida. There are forty-five days less rain at Malaga than at Nice, there being but twenty-nine in the former place; still there is this drawback, that the rainy season is confined to a short interval of a few weeks, while in other resorts it spreads over several months, a small quantity falling each day. Fires are necessary nearly every afternoon in the winter; and in the north rooms of the hotels, which are some ten degrees colder than the rooms with a southern exposure, they should be kept up all day. When either the terral or levanter is blowing, invalids should stay in-doors and keep warm.

Malaga is reached either by steamer from Naples or Gibraltar, or by sail from Madrid.

Ninety miles from Malaga, in a south-easterly direction, in Algeria, we have a climate which in many respects is in marked contrast to that of the former place. Malaga, as before stated, has an intensely dry atmosphere most of the year. In Algiers it is almost as constantly moist. The yearly rain-fall reaches as high as sixty-seven inches. The amount which falls in the winter months alone varies from thirty-six to forty inches. There are but two seasons in Algeria, viz., the winter and summer season; nearly all the rainy weather is in the winter. North-west and north-east winds prevail in the cold months. The mean annual temperature is sixty-four degrees F. In the month of January the temperature varies between forty-five and fifty-three degrees. The summer months are intensely hot; ninety-eight in the shade not being an unusual thing.

The climate of Algiers is essentially a moist

one; only those who improve in a moist atmosphere should go there.   A winter residence, from November until the middle of February, is of benefit in many forms of consumption, chronic bronchitis, and Bright's disease.

# CHAPTER XIV.

## CLIMATES OF FLORENCE AND ROME.

Florence in a hail-storm—Peculiarities of the prevalent winds —Sunshine—Sudden changes—Location of the city—Malarial fevers—Enteritis—Mean temperature of winter and summer months — Climate not suited for consumptive invalids—Rome—Roman fever—Effects of sight-seeing—Mortality among Americans—Safest time of the year to reside in Rome.

IT is not pleasant to arrive at your destination in a storm. And if you have been looking and longing for weeks, for blue skies and bright sunshine at the time when they ought to exist, and only get rain and hail-storms, and occasional glimpses of the sun through the windows of an Italian hotel or railway carriage, you would probably feel disgusted with the climate, with yourself and everybody who had ever spoken or written of the sunshine and bright skies of Italy. Such was our experience in the winter of 1872. We had been three weeks in Italy waiting for the rain to cease, for the floods to dry up, for the country to look something better than a vast swamp, when we started for Florence. At Pistoja the train came to a final stop on account of the broken bridges and mountain torrents, and we were forced to go around by way of Pisa, nearly one hundred miles out of the direct course of travel, to reach Florence. When the train arrived in the latter city, the rain which had accompanied us in all our sojournings changed to hail. The storm was terrific, and the cold penetrating, although the thermometer at the hotel only marked forty degrees F. Of course such an experience is not calculated to give one very high views of the health-giving properties of the climate. It is apt to develop one-sided criticism. But we have examined the subject carefully, looked into the health reports, weather reports, and mortuary records, have elicited the experience of other travellers sick and well, and the results destroy the reputation for healthfulness of a Florentine atmosphere. And were it not for the fact that there seems to be a general impression among Americans that Florence is a delightful winter residence, we would not have mentioned it, and only do so now to point out its eminent disadvantages as a home for invalids.

The city occupies the Valley of the Arno, in latitude forty-three degrees north. It is built on both sides of the river Arno, a narrow muddy stream, which scarcely deserves the name of river. When the tide is low the odor arising from its shores are anything but agreeable, or conducive to health. The Apennines rise up on the north, south, and west, but give little shelter to the valley. In the winter season the cold northern winds coming over the snow-capped mountains sweep through the valley, and suddenly change a warm sunshiny day to a disagreeably cold one. This cold wind is very penetrating. It has that peculiar coldness which all winds have that blow over snowy regions. The natural warmth of the atmosphere in the valley also makes this wind more disagreeable and injurious than it would otherwise be. You may go out in the morning and find the sky clear, and the sun bright and warm. Before noon these winds may blow down on the city, changing the atmosphere at once from the warmth of May to the coldness of February or

9

March.   These sudden changes characterize the climate of Florence in winter-time.   Every invalid who through necessity or choice is compelled to reside in Florence in winter, dreads the north wind. They cannot go out-of-doors while it lasts, and it is even as uncomfortable in-doors unless the house is artificially warmed.   The old palaces where so many visitors reside are exceedingly cheerless.   Their thick stone walls and small deep-set windows do not let in enough warmth or sunshine to dispel the gloom within.

Bronchial and intestinal troubles are quite common in Florence among strangers.   The sudden changes in the weather referred to are generally the cause of these disorders.   Some cases, however, may be referred to the senseless manner in which the majority of travellers do their sight-seeing.   From morning till night they keep up an incessant round of visits from churches to picture galleries, and down in  damp excavations among antediluvian ruins until nature gives way under the unaccustomed strain. Many a fine constitution has succumbed to the uncontrollable restlessness and anxiety to see and examine at once the accumulated art treasures of centuries. Malarial diseases are not common in Florence. A few who contract Roman fever in the south of Italy come to Florence to be nursed and treated before the disease has fully developed.

From meteorological records we learn that the mean temperature of October for a period of ten years was fifty-nine degrees; of November, forty-nine degrees; January, forty-one degrees F. The hottest month in summer is July, and the average mean of that month is seventy-six degrees: on the coldest day in January the mercury stood at twenty-nine degrees. The average rain-fall is thirty-five inches. Experienced travellers say that the best months for delicate persons to reside in Florence are October, May, and June. We would advise invalids to avoid the city at all times.

Our personal investigations into the climatic peculiarities of Rome were attended by the same unfavorable results. Although in the month of November, when the rainy season was supposed to be terminated, the city was drenched daily by fierce rain-storms, and the waters of the Tiber overflowed the lands and covered the streets in the lower portions of the city.   The thermometer ranged from forty-five to fifty degrees, but it felt much colder, especially when the wind came from the north.   The mean temperature for November during a period of twelve years was fifty-four degrees; of January, forty-six degrees; and the yearly rain-fall is said to average thirty-nine inches.   The climate in Rome, in December, January, and early part of February, is more equable than in either Naples or Florence.   There are fewer sudden changes.   Pulmonary complaints are often benefited during the period mentioned.   But the atmosphere in the modern city and the suburbs, towards the Campagna, is loaded at certain seasons with the most deadly miasm.   Even in the winter, when there is a comparative immunity from the poison, malarial fevers are continually occurring.   The Pontine marshes, which occupy the southern part of the *Campagna de Roma*, are the source of the miasm.   The marshy district was originally about thirty miles long, and varied from four to eleven miles in breadth.   It is separated from the sea-coast by a belt of trees.

Part of this region has been reclaimed, and drained at the expense of thousands of lives, but the remainder still generates the deadly mephitic vapors which make it dreaded by all. Those who inhabit the tillable portions only reside in their homes during the winter. In the summer they leave and seek the protection of the mountains. Although marshes which contain large quantities of decaying vegetable matters are the most prolific generators of miasmatic poison, there are other varieties of soil where it is often produced. It is found in dry sandy soil where the subsoil is composed of clay which prevents the water from being absorbed or drained away. Of course to produce miasm a certain amount of organic matter is necessary in connection with this kind of soil, but it is generally present. Where granite or trap rock is crumbling and disintegrating, or where the soil is formed of the débris of these rocks with a small proportion of organic matter, miasm is developed. Unless this variety of soil is disturbed, however, by excavations, the malaria it contains does no injury. As soon as building commences, remittent and intermittent fevers prevail extensively in their vicinity.  Dr. W. C. Maclean, in an article on miasmatic fevers, mentions the sudden outburst of these fevers in Hong Kong immediately following extensive excavations.  The soil of this island is composed of decaying granite, in which, in connection with the water it absorbs, a fungous growth is developed.  Fredal regards this fungus as bearing intimate relations to malaria, either itself being the cause of the fevers or at least assisting in forming the poison.  Mephitic vapor varies so much in character in different localities, that its composition is not well understood.  It is said to contain carburetted, phosphuretted, and sulphuretted hydrogen, and the débris of plants and insects.  Dr. Salsbury discovered in it a cryptogamic parasite, which he believes to be the direct cause of malarial fevers.  He caught some of the parasites on a glass, carried them to an elevated position, where malaria was unknown, and allowed a student to inhale the cryptogams; the result was a well-marked case of intermittent fever.  The malignity of remittent and intermittent fevers of Southern Italy arises from the fact that the marshy districts cover a large area of country, and under the heat of an Italian sun throw out their poisonous germs in great abundance. The pernicious form of malarial fever commonly known as Roman fever is probably the most fatal form of miasmatic disease. In Rome and other portions of Southern Italy, it carries off large numbers of the transient population, whether Italians or foreigners. Victor Emanuel's legislature, which holds its sessions in Rome, loses a number of its members every year from this disease. Among foreigners, however, it displays extraordinary virulence. The number of Americans who die in Rome and other parts of Italy from Roman fever is very great. Few have any conception of the extent of the mortality among strangers of all classes from this disease. As before remarked, the months of greatest freedom from malaria are December, January, and February. Even within this period the greatest care is required in eating, drinking, bathing and exercising. Until the stranger becomes acclimated he should observe his usual home custom in the number of his meals and their preparation, avoiding the light Roman breakfast of roll and coffee, and the late and heavy dinner. Walking and riding are good if not continued until the blood is overheated. In visiting the churches and other objects of interest, an extra shawl or cloak should be carried and worn when inside to keep out the cold air which is found in many of them. Passing from a warm light atmosphere into the damp chilly air of these places has planted the seeds of serious disease in many a careless traveller. All the sight-seeing and visiting should be done in daylight hours. After dark there is great danger in travelling about, as the night breezes often blow in from the Campagna, loaded with mephitic vapors in the neighborhood.

With regard to the selection of a residence, the same general rules given elsewhere are necessary. The healthiest places in Rome, are near the Esquiline and on the Via Condotti. Private lodgings may be had in these localities, which are as comfortable as one can expect who has been accustomed to the modern luxuries of a New York home.

# CHAPTER XV.

## THE ITALIAN LAKES.

Lake scenery—Peculiarities of lakes on Italian side of the mountains—Variations of climate on opposite sides of lakes—Protection from storms by the mountains—Lake Como—Scenery—Health resorts—Bellagio and Lakes Maggiore, Lugano, Iseo, and Garda.

THE Italian lakes have not attained to any special degree of importance as winter resorts for invalids. They are generally visited by tourists in the spring and fall months. Nevertheless, they possess a winter climate better suited to invalids than any other part of Italy, with the exception of the Riviera. They are protected on the north by the Alpine chain of mountains, close to which they lie, and on the east by " spurs " from these mountains. Being thus sheltered from the cold winds coming down from Northern Europe, and open to the south, the winter season is mild, and subject to few sudden thermal variations. The air is clear, pure, and bracing. Occa-

9*

sionally, as in all mountain lakes, storms suddenly spring up, bringing with them a cold wind which has an injurious effect on invalids who are exposed to its influence.   There are, however, many places along the shores which are affected but little by the cold. The average range of the thermometer in April is sixty degrees; in June, seventy-four degrees; in October, sixty-one, and in January fifty-two degrees. The diurnal variations in winter do not exceed twelve degrees.   Dr. Henry Bennet, of Mentone, considers the latter part of April, May and June as the best period for invalids to reside in the lake districts; but as the rain-fall in April is excessive, it cannot be a suitable month for the sick.   During December, January and February invalids who are not the subjects of advanced disease of the lungs, and who possess an average amount of health, can live comfortably in any of the villages on these lakes, and be considerably benefited by their sojourn.   Patients must keep in-doors whenever the cold winds come down from the mountains.   When out-of-doors they should be provided with sufficient extra clothing to keep from taking cold.   Extra clothing is necessary in any climate during winter, and especially in a warm one, where sudden changes of temperature are felt to a greater degree than in more northern and colder regions.

The Lake of Como is one of the largest of the Italian lakes. From the days of Pliny to the present time it has been renowned for the great beauty of its scenery, and its genial, mild and clear atmosphere. The lake resembles a river, being long and narrow. At its widest portion it measures two and a half miles, while in length it is thirty miles. It is about seven hundred feet above the sea-level. The peculiar characteristics of Italian scenery are found here in their highest perfection. Mountains precipitous in form and grand in outline, with their snow-covered tops peering above the clouds, guard the northern shore. Their slopes are covered with luxuriant groves of mulberry and olive-trees, and all along the shores white-walled villas peer out from among the groves and terraced gardens. There are many little villages on the shore, some from their position enjoying a milder climate than others. Varenna has a warm, sheltered situation, but Bellagio and Cadenallia are more re-sorted to by Americans. There are excellent hotels and private boarding-houses in these places, where the invalid and tourist can find every modern convenience.

Invalids who arrive at the Lake from the south in winter must not attempt the passage of the Alps before the warm spring weather appears.

Lake Maggiore, in point of scenery and climate, is inferior to Lake Como. It is protected on the south by the Alps, but is more exposed on the east. Sudden changes of temperature are more frequent here than at Lake Como, yet the winter all through is comparatively mild and pleasant.

Lake Iseo is probably more completely sheltered than the other Italian lakes, being surrounded on all sides by towering mountains. It is fourteen miles long, three wide, and is close to the Alps. Numerous villages are scattered up and down along the mountain slopes to the borders of the lake. Lovere, a town at the head of the lake, is frequently visited by invalids. Lady Mary Montague made this place

her home for a number of years.    Many physicians prefer Lake Iseo to the others as a health
resort.    As yet, however, it is not sufficiently fashionable to attract many visitors.

## FOR THE FALL OF 1874.

# NEW PUBLICATIONS

OF

# G. P. PUTNAM'S SONS.

AMONG THE TREES. By William Cullen Bryant. With numerous Illustrations by Jervis McEntee. Beautifully printed and bound. Square 8vo, cloth extra, full gilt, $3.50; full morocco, $7.00.

MOONFOLK. A True Account of the Home of the Fairy Tales. By Mrs. Jane G. Austin. With over 60 Illustrations, drawn and engraved on wood, by W. J. Linton. Small 8vo, cloth extra, $2.00.

EGYPT AND ICELAND IN THE YEAR 1874. With an Account of an Expedition to the Tyoom (never before printed). By Bayard Taylor. Square 16mo, cloth extra, $1.50; 12mo, uniform with the Household Edition of the Works, $1.50.

"The letters from Iceland by Bayard Taylor in *The New York Tribune* contain very interesting descriptions of that country and of the grand millennial festival which was celebrated there on the 6th and 7th of August. These letters have done more to draw attention to this remote part of the world than any other publications of our times. They describe the incidents of the voyage thither, including a visit to the Faroe Islands, and they abound in delineation of scenery and of life such as the common world is wholly unfamiliar with. They will undoubtedly be collected into a volume on Mr. Taylor's return to the United States, and when thus collected, they will form a most interesting addition to the long series of books of travel which he has given to the public."—*Providence Journal.*

GERMAN UNIVERSITIES. A Narrative of Personal Experience, and a Critical Comparison of the System of Higher Education in Germany with those of England and the United States. By Prof. Jas. Morgan Hart. 12mo, cloth extra, $1.75.

RECOLLECTIONS OF A TOUR IN SCOTLAND IN 1803. By Dorothy Wordsworth. The Journal of the famous Excursion made by Wm. Wordsworth and S. T. Coleridge. Edited by Principal Shairp. 12mo, cloth extra, $2.50.

" The volume glistens with charming passages, showing how rich in ' Wordsworthian ' fancy was this modest sister. We have to thank Dr. Shairp, and the thanks must be hearty, for now for the first time giving them a complete form."—*London Athenæum.*

" Many readers will turn with a pure delight from mental wars and questions, to wander amid the grandeur and beauty of Scottish glens and mountains, in the company of so bright a being as Dora Wordsworth, the loved and loving sister of the Poet.'* —*Windsor Gazette.*

NOTES ON ENGLAND AND ITALY. By Mrs. Hawthorne, (wife of the Novelist). New Illustrated Edition. Steel prints of Edinburgh, Peterborough Cathedral, Dumbarton Castle, Florence, the Coliseum, etc., etc. Printed on fine paper, handsomely bound in cloth, $5.00 ; morocco extra, $10.

" It is evident that the spirit of Hawthorne's genius has in some measure enshrouded his wife, and lent a bright lustre to her own thoughts."—*Syracuse Journal.*

" One of the most delightful books of travel that have come under our notice." —*Worcester Spy.*

" The grace and tenderness of the author of the ' Scarlet Letter ' is discernable in its pages."—*London Saturday Review.*

GEOMETRY AND FAITH. By Rev. Thos. Hill, D.D., LL.D., formerly President of Antioch College, and lately President of Harvard University. Square 12mo, cloth, $1.00.

" The writer shows in all his essays, a curious combination of the mathematical, metaphysical with the theological mind. He injects devoutness even into theorems and syllogisms."—*Boston Globe.*

RODDY'S ROMANCE. A Story for Young-folks. By *Helen Kendrick Johnson.* 16mo, cloth extra, $1.

THE GIRLHOOD OF SHAKESPEARE'S HEROINES. In a Series of Tales. By Mary Cowden Clarke. First and Second Series. Small 8vo, cloth extra, each, $2.00.

"Her imagination, retracing of influence and development is symmetrical, consistent, and skillful."—*N. Y. Evening Mail.*

LECTURE NOTES ON QUALITATIVE ANALYSIS. By Henry B. Hill, A.M., Assistant Prof. of Chemistry in Harvard University. 16mo, cloth, 75 cts.

SOPHISMS OF PROTECTION. By Frederic Bastiat. With Preface by Horace White. *Popular Manual Series.* 12mo, cloth, $1.00.

"Contains the most telling statements of the leading principles of the Free-trade theory, ever published, and is perhaps unsurpassed in the happiness of its illustrations." —*N. Y. Nation.*

HOW TO MAKE MONEY. By Geo. Cary Eggleston, Author of "How to Educate Yourself." *Handy Book Series.* 12mo, cloth, 75 cts. *In Press.*

INFANT DIET. By A. Jacobi, M.D., Clinical Professor of Diseases of Children, College of Physicians and Surgeons, New York. Revised and Enlarged by Mary Putnam Jacobi, M.D. *Handy Book Series.* 12mo, cloth, 75 cts.

ORTHOPÆDIA AND ITS TREATMENT. By James Knight, M.D. 8vo, cloth. Fully illustrated.

WINTER HOMES FOR INVALIDS. A complete account of the various Localities in America and Europe, suitable for Consumptives and Invalids during the Winter Months ; with Special Reference to the Climatic Variations in each place, and their Influence upon Disease. By Joseph W. Howe, M.D. Author of "Emergencies," "The Breath," etc., etc. 12mo, cloth. *In Press.*

MUSIC AND ITS INFLUENCE ON HEALTH AND DISEASE. Translated from French of Chomet, by Mrs. Laura A. Flint. 12mo, cloth extra. *In Press.*

‡ **BRISTED. Five Years in an English University.** By Charles Astor Bristed, late Foundation Scholar of Trinity College, Cambridge. Fourth edition. Revised and amended by the author. 12mo, cloth, extra, $2.50.

A new edition of this standard work, for some years out of print, has long been called for. With its facts and statistics corrected, and brought down to recent date, the volume conveys to the college graduate or undergraduate information of special value and importance, while the vivid and attractive record of a personal experience contains much to interest the general reader.

"It is characterized by most excellent taste, and contains a great deal of most novel and interesting information."—*Philadelphia Inquirer.*

**BRYANT. Letters of a Traveller.** By William Cullen Bryant. With steel portrait. New edition. 12mo, cloth, $2.

——— **Letters From the East.** Notes of a Visit to Egypt and Palestine. 12mo, cloth, $1.50.

——— The Same. Illustrated edition. With fine engravings on steel. 12mo, cloth extra, $2.50.

——— **Orations and Addresses.** Including those delivered on Irving, Cooper, Cole, Verplanck, Shakespeare, Morse, Scott, etc. 12mo, cloth $2.

**BEST READING, THE. A Classified Bibliography for Easy Reference.** With Hints on the Selection of Books; on the Formation of Libraries, Public and Private; on Courses of Reading, etc.; a Guide for the Librarian, Bookbuyer, and Bookseller. The Classified Lists, arranged under about 500 subject headings, include all the most desirable books now to be obtained either in Great Britain or the United States, with the published prices annexed. Revised Edition. 12mo, paper, $1.00. Cloth, $1.50,

" The best work of the kind we have seen."— *College Courant.*

"We know of no manual that can take its place as a guide to the selection of a library."—*N. Y. Independent.*

† **BLACKWELL. Studies in General Science.** By Antoinette Brown Blackwell. 12mo (uniform with Child's " Benedicite"). Cloth extra $2.25.

" The writer evinces admirable gifts both as a student and thinker. She brings a sincere and earnest mind to the investigation of truth."—*N. Y. Tribune.*

"The idea of the work is an excellent one, and it is ably developed."—*Boston Transcript.*

† **BLAKE. The Production of the Precious Metals; or, Statistical Notices of the Principal Gold and Silver Producing Regions of the World.** With a chapter upon the Unification of Gold and Silver Coinage. By Wm. P. Blake, Commissioner from the State of California to the Paris Exposition of 1867. One volume, 8vo, cloth extra, $2.50.

Milton Keynes UK
Ingram Content Group UK Ltd.
UKHW040929180224
437992UK00003B/113